A Fighter Named Death

When some strongarm hoods try to muscle in on the fight game, hefty Joe Puma is hired to find out who's doing the dirty work.

What looks like a typical rackets murder turns out to be a dangerous deal for the private eye. He tussles with some trigger-happy punks and a couple of lethal beauties.

Then in one quick leap from mattress to mat he finds himself in a clinch with a murderer who's still fighting, still hating, still bent . . . on the kill.

the hundred dollar girl

William Campbell Gault

Adams Media
New York London Toronto Sydney New Delhi

Adams Media
An Imprint of Simon & Schuster, Inc.
57 Littlefield Street
Avon, Massachusetts 02322

For information about special discounts for bulk purchases, please contact Simon & Schuster Special Sales at 1-866-506-1949 or business@simonandschuster.com.

Manufactured in the United States of America

ISBN 978-1-4405-5792-7
ISBN 978-1-4405-3912-1 (ebook)

This work has been previously published in print format as a Signet Book by The New American Library of World Literature, Inc., New York, NY.

chapter one

His achievements in the ring never measured up to his tabloid bedroom reputation, but that didn't make him a prelim boy. He had a lot of friends and he picked up too many tabs. He had an abundance of physical courage, and a bad manager can turn that virtue into a vice quickly enough by simply matching his boy beyond his current skill and experience.

His name was Terry Lopez and there's a combination for you, Mexican-Irish. A handsome bastard, a middleweight. He had a wife the local papers called a "former starlet." In this case, it simply meant she had a five-line part in a "B" picture a few years back. Before she changed her name to Lopez, it had been Gallegher, Bridget Gallegher, so if they had had any kids, they'd have been three-quarters Irish.

No kids. He was out for laughs and she rode with it for a while. He got into the top ten rating in *Ring* for a brief spell and that gave him a few big-money bouts but he had no inclination toward saving. That brought him up to the Hans Mueller bout broke and in debt.

That brought his wife into my office.

Bridget Gallegher Lopez had red hair that looked natural to me. Her nose was a little too blunt to be classic but it fitted the face, which was pure lace-curtain Irish. There is a class to this segment of the nationality that belies its origins, and she had that kind of class. It is not Philadelphia or Boston, understand, but only a shade under it.

She told me I had been recommended to her by Sid Schwartz, a criminal attorney I knew.

"And why?" I asked.

"Because of my husband," she answered. "Do you know who he is?"

5

I nodded. "I've seen him fight. Twice. This next one is his biggest one to date, I'd say. Wouldn't you?"

She licked her lips. "Yes." She took a breath. "It's a—step, as Terry says. I mean, toward the championship, the first *big* step."

"It could easily be," I agreed, and wondered to myself who the other woman was, the woman she had come to have me check, undoubtedly.

"Why are you smiling?" she asked.

"I didn't know I was," I said. "Sorry."

"You're thinking," she guessed, "that I've come to see you about some—some floozie Terry's mixed up with."

I lied with a shake of the head.

"It's not anything like that," she went on. "It's—money."

"In your husband's trade," I said, "it always is. I think you came to the wrong man, Mrs. Lopez."

She stared at me quizzically.

"I'm a one-man office," I said. "Can I fight the major mobsters?"

"I haven't asked you to fight anyone," she pointed out quietly.

"You haven't," I agreed. "I apologize again. I should listen more and talk less."

"I have all the fighter I need," she said. "I'm looking for an investigator. Isn't that what you are, Mr. Puma?"

"In my limited but determined way," I admitted.

She met my gaze candidly. "Perhaps you've checked our credit and prefer not to accept me as a client."

I stared at her and didn't answer. I thought her chin quivered. Her voice did. "Is that it?"

"Is that what?"

She lifted her chin. She had a lovely neck. "You don't seem to be—overeager to accept my patronage."

"I haven't checked your credit," I told her. "If I believed what I read in the newspapers, it must be bad, but I don't usually believe the newspapers. I get a lot of bad credit risks as clients in my profession and collect from most of them."

"I'm sorry," she said. "I suppose I expected more—salesmanship from you, but then, you're not an automobile salesman, are you?"

"I've been called some despicable things," I said, "but never that. Why don't you tell me your problem, Mrs. Lopez? I promise to keep my big mouth shut until you've finished."

"It's the Hans Mueller fight," she said. "I think he's going to throw it." She paused. "Terry doesn't—confide in me, but I don't think it's his idea. He likes to win, that boy. But his manager—do you know him?"

"Gus Galbini? I've met him twice, I think."

"I don't like him," she said. "I think he's a crook."

I shrugged. "His reputation isn't much worse or better than most managers'. Boxing's infested with crooks."

"Terry isn't crooked," she said. "Except when it comes to women, Terry plays it straight all the way." She flushed and looked away from me.

I said, "You accept that? You must love him."

She was still blushing, but her gaze came back to meet mine. "At first, I thought he was going somewhere; I went along for the ride. And then——" she shrugged. "Call it animal magnetism. I've overlooked some pretty raw—escapades."

"You mean, at first you thought he was going to make a lot of money, and that was the attraction?"

She nodded and looked at me quietly.

"Well, then," I said, "what's wrong with throwing a fight? A lot more money is made on fixed fights, you know."

She was silent.

"Do you want to be more frank?" I asked quietly.

"I didn't come in here, Mr. Puma, to hire you to investigate *me*. My motives are cloudy even to me. I want you to investigate Gus Galbini."

"In what way? Do you mean in regard to the Mueller fight?"

"In that way and all the ways," she said. A pause. "Gus Galbini seems to know every gambler and *every chippie* in town. I want you to investigate his influence on Terry."

And every chippie. . . . That's what was bugging her. The fixed fight gambit had been only to save face. The dames were what was bothering Mrs. Terry Lopez.

But she hadn't asked me to check her husband, which I wouldn't have done, not for infidelity. Galbini was my target and I could use the business. It had been a slow month.

"His credit, too?" I asked her.

"Everything," she said. She smiled and stood up. "But not *our* credit. Do you usually get a retainer?"

"I'll bill you," I said. And thought, in my lecherous way: *One way or another, you'll pay!*

She went out, leaving some perfume behind. I sat there, pondering on philanderers. So often, they had beauties like Bridget for wives. And still they went to Newcastle for their coal.

Except for the credit report, investigating Gus Galbini was not a chore that suggested the direct approach. I went down to the old two-door and drove over to Delamater's. Delamater's is a gym and health studio out on Olympic where a number of fighters train.

And also a place where a number of wise guys hang out, including some gamblers, big and little. The hoodlum involvement in boxing was getting a lot of current publicity, but it had always existed in this country. Boxing had been born in the saloon district, it had achieved the salons, but it was still a mugs' game.

Barney Delamater ran a two-faced store. The gym, which fronted on Olympic, was barnlike, old and gray, weathered stucco and faded redwood. The health studio connected with this but fronted on Eighteenth, all white tile and shining plate glass set in polished aluminum casements. Barney rarely came over to this newer section; his origins were humble and his tastes simple.

He was in the gym, in a littered, glass-enclosed corner office from where he could view each of his three rings and all the multitudinous light and heavy bags and other paraphernalia of his shop.

He's bald and short and jovial and he grinned at me when I came into his office. "Decided to listen to me?" he asked.

It was an old private joke. In a bar fight, I had decked one of the local promising heavyweights a few years back. Ever since, Barney had insisted I had a future in the ring.

"Listen to you?" I answered. "On some subjects, I will."

He leaned back in his office chair and smiled at me, waiting.

"On Terry Lopez, for instance," I said. "How good is he?"

Barney shrugged. "He's no Greb."

"Nobody ever was, except for Greb. Is Lopez good enough for that German?"

"Hans Mueller?" He shrugged again. "Who can tell, with them foreigners? They build up a big rep on stumblebums, come over here—and get clobbered."

"Not Mueller," I said. "He's been in this country a long time. He's beat some pretty good boys."

"That he has," Barney agreed. "Why the interest?"

"I'd like to get a bet down," I said. "I can always use an easy buck. Which way should I bet?"

"You're lying," he said mildly. He leaned forward. "You heard something, huh?"

I stared at him. He stared at me.

"From Gus?" he asked quietly.

"Galbini? We're not that close."

"Who, then?"

"Maybe, just maybe, from somebody very close to Terry Lopez."

"His wife," he said. "That's it. She came to you?"

We went through another staring session.

Barney said, "Good-looking girl, isn't she?"

I didn't answer.

Barney leaned back in his chair again, and his voice was musing. "A model, I guess she used to be. Though I got it on real good authority that she wasn't above answering a call, now and then, if the caller pleased her. At one grand a night, I heard. *One thousand dollars for one night.*" He shook his head wonderingly. "Now, who'd pay that, when you can get a good steak for five bucks?"

I said, "Somebody who had one thousand and five dollars, I suppose, Barney. You're old, don't forget."

"I'm not old," he said peevishly, "and I was never young enough to be that dumb."

Another silence. He stared at his desk and I stared at him. He looked up. "So? What else is new?"

"Don't you want to talk about the Mueller-Lopez fight?"

"I don't know anything about it," he said. "It looks like you know more than I do about that."

"What kind of man is Gus Galbini?"

"He's a manager. A manager is what he has to be if he wants to make a buck. And they all want to make a buck, any way they can."

"They can't all be crooked, Barney."

"Everybody has to eat," he said. "Hardly anybody is crooked unless there's a buck in it."

Another pause. And I said, "Okay, let's say it's all on the level. Who would you pick, Mueller or Lopez?"

"Mueller," he said firmly. "He trains. He keeps in shape. He runs on the road, not after dames."

I winked at him. "Thanks. That's the way I'll bet, then."

"Bet," he said scornfully. "Who do you think you're kidding? Come on, Joe—you heard something, right?"

"Nothing I've confirmed," I said. "When I do, if there's a buck in it, I'll tell you." And then I remembered what Bridget had told me. I asked, "Is it true that Galbini knows every gambler and every chippie in town?"

"He knows a lot of both," Barney conceded. "He introduced Lopez to his wife."

Through the glass behind him, now, I could see someone entering the center ring. It was a blond head in a flat-top cut and though his back was to me, I was almost sure it was

Hans Mueller. He had the bunched hitting muscles near his shoulder blades, and the thick German neck.

Barney turned to look where I was looking. "Mueller," he said. "Watch him work out, why don't you? And then make your bet."

I thanked him for nothing and went out and over toward the center ring. A Negro who looked close to the light-heavy class was climbing between the ropes in the far corner from Mueller. He had a Fitzimmons build, slim legs and enormous shoulders. He appeared to be three inches taller than Mueller.

I went over to stand next to a two-bit bookie I knew slightly. I asked him, "Who's the tall boy?"

"Lincoln Jones," he said. "All left hand and glass jaw."

"How did you figure this Mueller with Lopez?"

He shrugged. "If Lopez would train, he'd murder him. But when did Lopez ever take a fight serious enough to train?"

Jones was wearing a headgear but his opponent evidently scorned such a sissy protection. A very calm and confident-looking man, Hans Mueller.

At the bell, Jones came out erectly in an almost classic stance, stabbing with the left and moving to the right, away from Mueller's right.

But the German also had a hook and he moved in with it, landing heavily to Jones's ribs, crowding him. Jones tied him up.

They broke—and the German put his weight into a sneak right hand. It landed high on the head guard but the force of it sent Jones stumbling to his right. Hans Mueller moved in.

For ten seconds, he thudded rights and lefts into the taller man's belly, driving him up against the ropes, bulling him with his right shoulder, keeping him off balance while he went to work downstairs.

It was rough work at spar-mate's wages; Jones grunted a protest and looked toward his corner.

At the same time Mueller backed off and threw another flat-footed right hand. Jones went down.

Next to me, the two-bit bookie murmured, "Real storm trooper, huh? I'll bet he would have loved Hitler."

"He looks muscle-bound," I said. "Lopez could make him look clumsy, too."

The bookie sniffed. "Lopez! He's a lover, not a fighter. What's your interest in this, Puma?"

"Financial," I said. "I have to make a buck some way. Do you know Gus Galbini very well?"

The bookie shook his head, staring at me thoughtfully. "What's cooking?"

"Nothing," I said innocently. "I'm not on the inside of anything."

Jones was up now, standing quietly in one corner of the ring, while in another corner Mueller's handler was talking to him. Then the handler stepped out and the fighters moved toward the center of the ring again.

The bookie said, "If you're looking for Galbini, there he is." He nodded toward Barney's office.

I turned to see Gus Galbini going in and Barney rising to meet him. I thought Barney glanced toward me before shaking Galbini's outstretched hand.

I turned back to the ring to see that Mueller was letting up, pulling his punches a little. And leaning against the apron of the ring beyond this one, I saw another familiar face.

It was Terry Lopez, in street clothes. He was watching the action in this ring carefully, his face thoughtful. I went over there.

"I don't think you know me," I said. "My name is Joe Puma."

He nodded. "I've seen you around. Barney's mentioned you. I guess you know Gus, too, don't you?"

"I've met him," I said. "How does Mueller look to you?"

He smiled and shrugged. He was a handsome man, with jet-black hair and soft brown eyes. His face was unmarked.

"Were you here when he put Jones down?" I asked.

"Yup." He smiled again. "I'm not Jones." He looked at me lazily. "Are you a betting man, Mr. Puma?"

"At times," I said. "When I need the money." I paused. "And the risk isn't too great."

He stared at me steadily. "There's always a risk. Anything can happen in a ring, *anything*."

I returned his stare. "In other words, it would be a bad fight to bet on?"

He studied me quietly for a few seconds before saying, "All fights are bad bets. Stick to the ponies." He turned away and walked over toward the corner office, where his manager was still talking to Barney.

In the center ring, Jones and Mueller were only going through the motions, now; I went out and climbed into the car and headed for Venice, for the lower-class lodging of Snip Caster.

At one time, Snip had been a slicker, a confidante of the major mobsters, a dashing and articulate dandy.

Booze had got to him and from there he went to wine, as

his fortunes diminished. He now lived in a lodging house run by a lady named Aggie, a former madame who had outlived her saleability.

He was in the side yard of this lady's lean-to, ragged shorts and no shirt, getting the sun on an old army blanket laid over the gray Bermuda lawn. He looked drawn and sick.

Aggie, fortunately, was not in sight. I asked my friend, "What's the matter? Nothing serious, I hope?"

He shrugged and shivered, and put a hand on his bare abdomen.

"Muscatel stomach?" I suggested.

"Nope," he said. "Aggie's cooking, maybe. Jeepers, she's getting sloppy." He looked down at his white, stringy legs. "I sure don't look like a native, huh? I look like a tourist. Man, when I think of how I used to look in Palm Springs—" He glanced around. "You—bring a bottle?"

"I brought you a buck," I said. "You can get your own bottle and have forty-one cents left over."

"A buck," he said scornfully. *"Big, big man—a buck!"*

"Maybe five later, if you come up with something," I said.

"Five—phooie," He rubbed his stomach.

"Gus Galbini," I said, "and the Mueller-Lopez fight. That's what I'd like the word on."

He rubbed his stomach some more and looked out at the gray grass. "Gus Galbini— That son-of-a-bitch! He's the bastard that ruined Joey Veller. Joey should have been featherweight champ. Hell, he beat the champ, in Mexico."

"Gus sold him out?"

Snip grimaced. "Who knows? In that division, there's no big money riding, so it doesn't have to be spread. And on those local fixes, how many have to know?"

"Snip," I said, "you've really got nothing on Gus, then, have you?"

"For a dollar," he said, "what do you want? If I was active, if I could get around, I could ask some old friends. But I wouldn't want 'em to come here and see Aggie, guy like me, with the broads I used to shack with. I got *some* pride left, don't forget."

It was one of his petulant days, his reminiscent days. I said nothing, being patient.

"Galbini," he said, and looked again at the gray grass. "Nah, I don't think he's got any tie-ups. Lopez, now—he's got that sister."

"What sister?"

"Don't you remember? The one that got all that ink when

Bugsy Martin went to the gas chamber? Remember, she claimed they were engaged and all."

"I remember now," I said. "But her name was Loper, not Lopez, Mary Loper. She was a model, right?"

"She was a model," Snip agreed, "and she called herself Loper. So she's still Terry's sister and who says she can't change one letter in her last name?"

"Are you sure she's Lopez' sister?" I asked.

"One will get you five," he said. "And Bugsy Martin was no bush league hood, either. There's your angle, if you're looking for a big money tie-up."

I shook my head doubtfully. "I never once, in all that publicity, remember her being mentioned as the sister of Terry Lopez."

"Jesus!" Snip shook his head, too. "Man—is that how you stay hep, reading the newspapers? Check it, check it. Everybody knows it, except maybe newspaper readers. Where's the fin?"

I took out my wallet. It contained two fives and three singles. "I'm kind of low, Snip," I explained. "I wonder if—"

"You're not as low as I am," he reminded me. "Come on— I want to get off the grape and back onto corn and it takes a fin—"

"Okay," I said, and that left me eight dollars. "If you learn any more—"

"I'll ask around," he promised. "As soon as this bellyache goes away, I'll ask around. Cripes, I'm not rich enough to have ulcers, am I?"

"You should see a doctor, Snip," I told him quietly. "You can owe him. Everybody owes doctors."

chapter two

A REPORTER I KNEW HAD THE CURRENT ADDRESS OF MARY Lopez Loper and I drove out to West Los Angeles on the off chance that she might be home.

It was a one-level triplex just outside of the Cheviot Hills section, a low and attractive building of antiqued barn siding and heavy shakes with a separate patio for each unit.

Miss Loper had the rear unit and the nicest patio, of red brick with a view of the hills to the east and the distant ocean to the south. She, like Snip Caster, was taking advantage of the sun but there was nothing flaccid or pale about the skin she exposed.

She was lying on an aluminum chaise longue with a floral and white pad, in a Bikini and all the flesh in sight was a golden brown. Her hair was a sun-bleached brown, her eyes as brown and soft as her brother's.

She was a thin girl but not in any sense emaciated. She looked up to see me staring at her and for a moment she seemed startled.

"Joe Puma is my name," I said. "I'm a private investigator."

She rose to a sitting position. "Oh? And?"

"I'd like to talk with you about your brother."

The brown eyes clouded and then glazed over. "My brother?"

I nodded. "Terry Lopez."

She took a breath. She paused, and then said, "Not many people know he is my brother. Who told you?"

"A friend of mine. I'd rather not mention his name."

"Well," she said, after a second, "it is a change. I mean, to have a snooper interested in somebody besides me. You're not a reporter, are you?"

14

I shook my head. "Scout's honor. It's the Mueller-Lopez fight I'd like to talk about."

"I don't know anything about it," she said. "Is it supposed to be—fixed, crooked?"

"At least one person thinks so," I said. I came over to sit on the other chaise longue.

She swung her feet around and lowered them to the ground. She leaned forward to stare at me and her slim halter afforded very little coverage. I averted my eyes.

She smiled, and sat more erectly. "One person thinks so? One person named what?"

"One nameless person," I answered. "Do you know Gus Galbini very well?"

"I know him. But surely he isn't talking about a fixed fight?"

"Not to my knowledge. What do you think of Gus?"

She frowned. "I don't really know him well enough to have an opinion on him. The—few times we met, he didn't impress me."

I paused and then asked, "Was he a—friend of Bugsy Martin's?"

She stared at me for seconds. "That was below the belt, wasn't it?"

"Not intentionally. I was looking for a—tie-up."

She said nothing, glaring at me.

"If a fight of this importance is going to be fixed," I explained gently, "it would be fixed only for important money. And that means the money would have to be spread around more than locally. It would imply the use of some—some organization, a syndicate. So far as I can learn, Gus Galbini isn't involved with any syndicate." I took a breath. "So, investigation being my business, I had to investigate any possible connection, however remote."

She said nothing.

"Doesn't that make sense?" I asked. "Believe me, I'm not here to cause you any trouble."

She licked her lips, started to say something, and then must have decided against it.

"I'll go," I said, after a few seconds. "Somehow, I've given you the wrong idea of why I'm here. I apologize for that." I started to get up.

"Wait," she said. "Sit down and relax, Mr. Puma."

I sat down and looked at her patiently.

She licked her lips again. "I—never thought of Sal as a—a mobster."

"Sal?"

"The man you call Bugsy. The man everybody calls Bugsy,

Salvadore Peter Martino, called Bugsy Martin. I never met any of his friends who looked like racketeers. When he——died, and the papers wrote those horrible stories about me, it was as though they were writing about somebody else." She broke off, staring at the patio.

"He was a big man," I said, "but he came up through the mobs and there was no reason to think he ever left them."

"I believe that," she said. And added, "Now."

A silence and she went on. "He knew Gus Galbini. Gus introduced him to me."

"And your brother to his wife," I added. "Is that all Gus knows—models?"

She lifted her eyebrows. "Models? Are you referring to Bridget Gallegher Lopez as a model?"

"Wasn't she?"

Mary Loper shrugged. "So all right, if that's your name for it."

"Let me put it this way—did she *ever* do any modeling?"

"To my knowledge, and I know the ones who are working, she never did any professional modeling. But she's my brother's wife and if she wants to call her old profession modeling, I won't argue with it."

Her face had been stiff and her voice strained as she said this. She seemed embarrassed when she'd finished.

I smiled. "You don't like her, huh?"

She said slowly, "I suppose, if she wasn't married to my brother, I'd like that girl. I guess I don't have much feeling about her, one way or the other."

I had learned what I had come to learn; Gus Galbini had known Bugsy Martin and that was a tenuous mob tie-up. There wasn't much more I was likely to learn here; why did I linger?

"Don't stare at me like that," she said.

"I'm sorry." I looked away, toward the hills.

After a few seconds, she asked, "What were you thinking about, when you were staring at me?"

"Of Salvadore Peter Martino, alias Bugsy Martin. Don't you believe he deserved the gas chamber?"

She hesitated, then said quietly, "I don't believe anybody does. And I don't think Sal killed that girl."

The woman she referred to as "that girl" had been a witness to a shooting in a Valley restaurant frequented by hoodlums. She had been killed two nights later. And the slugs recovered from her body had matched a gun traced to Bugsy Martin.

To me, that had been the weakest link in the D.A.'s case.

Because no professional would use a gun that could be in any way connected with him. And Bugsy had been no amateur.

But the jury had been and Bugsy had died in the gas chamber.

"What are you thinking about?" she asked again.

"The same—Salvadore Peter Martino. He ran into a real tiger of a D.A., didn't he?"

She sighed. "Yes. Sal's lawyer didn't want to take a chance on a jury, but Sal insisted." She grimaced. "Sal had a lot of confidence in his own—charm."

With reason, I thought. *With reason, if he charmed you, Mary Loper Lopez.*

I rose and looked down at her, all brown, flesh, eyes, and hair. If she was still mourning Bugsy Martin, it was not evident to my untrained observation.

I said, "Thanks. Can you think of anything else to tell me that might help?"

"No. But I'll talk with Terry, if you want to phone back. Terry rarely lies to me. Wouldn't that be the easiest way to learn if a fight is crooked?"

I smiled. "It would be, if the fighters were honest. But if they were honest, there wouldn't be any need to ask, would there?"

"I'll ask him, anyway," she said. She paused. Coquettishly? She paused, anyway, and said, "And then I'll call you."

I said, with warm and simple dignity, "I'll look forward to your call."

I went back to my car thinking of all that beautiful brown, wondering how a lovely like Mary Loper could have settled for a creep like Bugsy Martin. Women had the most unpredictable tastes. . . .

In the car, I sat for a moment, reviewing my labors up to now. I had asked a lot of questions, but what had I learned? Only that Gus Galbini had known Bugsy Martin.

Bugsy was dead; there was no line of inquiry open there.

It wasn't far from here to the address Bridget Gallegher Lopez had given me. I drove over.

It was a small new home on an expensive lot in the hills above Westwood. The semiclassic redhead was home. She opened the front door and said, "Well, hello! News already?"

"Very little," I said. "I did learn that Galbini knew Bugsy Martin." I paused. "And also that Gus introduced you to your husband."

Her pause was longer than mine had been. Then she said, "Come in and tell me what this all means."

I came into a paneled living room with a high-hearth fireplace, furnished in expensive contemporary.

"Drink?" she asked.

I shook my head, holding her gaze.

She didn't move. "Who did you ask about Bugsy Martin?"

"His former girl friend."

"Mary?"

I nodded.

Bridget Gallegher Lopez sighed and went over to sit on a pastel yellow love seat. She looked at the floor as she said, "Mary hates me, doesn't she?"

"I doubt it. I'm not here to relay family gossip, Mrs. Lopez."

"Mary hates me," she said, more vehemently this time.

I ignored that. I said quietly, "Now, why don't you tell me *all* you know about Galbini, and maybe I'll be better equipped to help."

She looked up. "Help?"

"To frame him, nail him, expose him—whatever you had in mind when you came to my office."

Her chin went up and her blue eyes glistened. "You don't need to be insulting. You've been listening to Mary. She sold you, didn't she?"

I said nothing.

"I tried to be friends with Mary," she went on. "Frankly, I like her. We—we could enjoy each other. But she hates me."

I made no comment.

The girl was working herself into a rage, now. "Loper—huh! Ashamed of her real name. Ashamed of her brother and hates his wife. What is she, a saint? A woman who lived with Bugsy Martin? Of all the slimy people I've ever met, that Bugsy Martin was the slimiest. Who does she think she—"

"When did you meet Bugsy?" I interrupted.

She glared at me. "What difference does it make?"

I shrugged. "I can never be sure what difference anything makes. I just go along asking questions until the light starts to break through."

She took a breath and said, "You don't have to ask any more questions for me. Just send me a bill for today and forget you ever saw me."

I stood up, and smiled down at her. "All right, though it won't be easy. Good luck, Mrs. Lopez."

"*Good*bye!" she said hoarsely.

I went out thoroughly dismissed.

Business picked up the next day and I had no time to think of the Lopez-Galbini-Martino axis for a while. But it must have been milling around in my subconscious, because when the Lopez-Mueller bout came up on a warm Friday evening, I was there in the fifth row.

Fights usually bore me these days, ineffectual clowns pawing at each other in TV farces. But Lopez, in shape, was a first-class mauler. And the German seemed to have the nasty instincts a real fighter is born with.

Unfortunately, Lopez wasn't in shape. If Mueller had been less cautious, it would have been a short fight, because Mueller was always in shape. But Terry Lopez came out for the first round like a Golden Glover, full of swings and scorning defense.

He had the crowd up and screaming. For less than a second, the German lost his poise—and was tagged with a sucker right hand.

It wasn't a button shot, but he was caught off balance and stumbled to one knee. The ref made him take an eight count. The fans went crazy and I looked over to the second row on the south side of the ring to see that Bridget Gallegher Lopez was up on her feet with the rest of Terry's fans, shrieking to her boy to finish off Hans Mueller.

The German wasn't that fragile. He was fully conscious through the count, taking it on one knee. Then he got up, went into his shell, and put his methodical mind to work, looking for flaws and signs of fatigue.

It was a dull third round to me, though Lopez' fans didn't seem to find it dull. Every time Terry threw the big miss, they screamed—and seemed to overlook the hooks Mueller sank into Terry's belly as he stepped inside the big miss.

Terry's speed began to diminish; he went into a left-hand paw and run, as the early rounds wore on. Then, in the sixth, Mueller belted him with a smashing right hand under the heart and I knew Lopez had no starch left.

He ran, he danced, he even clowned. But the German stalked him steadily, putting that hook into the belly, throwing that inside right to the heart.

Terry's smile was painful and his guard came down to protect his reddened stomach. Now, I thought, Mueller can get the button shot he's been setting up.

Twice, in the ninth, the German had a clear chance to end it, and both times he refused the opportunity. Terry was going on instinct now; he had nothing left but his guts.

It would have been a simple act of mercy if Mueller had

ended it with the big one; but he seemed intent on vengeance, on punishment. He saved the Sunday punch for the last thirty seconds of the last round.

On the floodlighted canvas, Lopez didn't even stir. I looked over to see the shock and dismay on the face of Bridget Gallegher Lopez. Then I got up and hurried out to the clean air.

I thought of what that two-bit bookie had told me at Barney Delamater's gym. This Hans Mueller was a storm trooper, a tough and insulated man.

In a sense it had been just punishment for a man who took his training as lightly as Terry Lopez, but it had looked too deliberate to me, too vengeful.

I stopped off for a couple of drinks before going home, and got into bed about eleven o'clock. Four hours later, at the ridiculous hour of three in the morning, my doorbell rang steadily and disturbingly.

I came up out of the fog of a licentious dream and stumbled, cursing, to the door to look into the belligerent face of Detective Sergeant Marty Dugan of the West Los Angeles Station.

"What in hell," I asked him, "can be important enough to bring you here at this hour?"

"The Mueller-Lopez fight," he answered. "Should I wait inside, or have you got some broad here for the night?"

"Come in, come in," I said. "What about the Mueller-Lopez fight?"

He came in, looked around at my slovenly housekeeping with a married man's disdain, and said, "You tell me what about it. You were investigating it a while back. Was it fixed and who fixed it?"

"I didn't learn much," I told him, "and what I learned can wait until daylight. You must be drunk, Marty. What's the big rush? What makes it important right *now?*"

"Gus Galbini," he said. "He was killed about an hour ago, murdered."

chapter three

THERE WASN'T ANY REASON FOR HIM TO DRAG ME DOWN TO the West Los Angeles Station; I could have told him all I knew in five minutes. But he insisted that Captain Apoyan wanted to see me, so I went along down to Purdue Street.

Flash bulbs flared and reporters crowded around as we came into the station.

Marty steered me past the reporters, ignoring their questions and smiling at their gibes. He hated them personally but needed them politically; he smiled us all the way to Captain Apoyan's office.

There, he closed the door, and cursed under his breath. Apoyan was talking to another detective and he looked up and frowned.

"Here's your man, Captain," Marty Dugan said. "Will you want me in here?"

Apoyan nodded and looked at Marty for seconds before shifting his gaze to me. "Well," he said, "what's your story?"

"I don't have any," I said. "If you've got questions, ask them." I lit a cigarette and came over to sit in a chair near his desk.

His face stiffened and he glared at me. The other detective asked quietly, "Is that all, Captain?"

Apoyan nodded without looking at him and the man left. Dugan sat in a chair near the door.

Finally, Apoyan said, "I don't need any of your insolence, Puma."

"And I don't need any of your official arrogance," I answered. "I was pulled out of bed at a ridiculous hour and brought down here for no reason. The only assumption I can make is that you brought me here to question me. I'm waiting."

21

"Maybe you'd rather wait in a cell," he suggested softly.

"If it has a bed in it, I certainly would."

His smile was cold. "Persecution— You hot-headed Italians and your persecution complexes—"

"Huh!" I said. "And you Armenians who get a badge and turn into Turks—"

His face drained. Even his lips seemed colorless. "Easy. You're not that big, Puma. You watch your damned tongue!"

"And you yours," I said. I looked at Marty. "Show me the cell. I'm ready."

Marty yawned, stood up, and looked at the captain.

"Sit down," Apoyan told him quietly. He looked at me for a few seconds. Then, "A little while back, you investigated the possibility of the Lopez-Mueller fight being fixed, didn't you?"

"Not exactly. I investigated Gus Galbini's possible tie-ups with people who could spread the money *if* the fight was fixed."

"Who hired you to investigate that?"

I hesitated and said, "Mrs. Lopez." I paused. "She pulled me off the case before I had learned much."

"Did you learn anything?"

I told him what I had learned, including the Bugsy Martin bit.

Interest came to his eyes and he looked at Dugan meaningfully. He asked me, "And why did she pull you off the case?"

"I don't know. Possibly because of my arrogance. She didn't like some of the things I told her."

He leaned back in his chair and studied me thoughtfully. "Mary Loper, eh? That's Lopez' sister?"

I nodded.

"Does she live on the west side?"

I nodded. "Near Cheviot Hills. If you pick her up, Captain, I'd appreciate it if you don't mention where you got her name."

He nodded absent-mindedly. "And Mrs. Lopez was suspicious of Galbini?"

"That's right. Though it was through Galbini she met her husband."

He looked at Sergeant Dugan. "Pick her up. And send Preston in here to take Puma's statement."

Dugan went out and Apoyan looked back at me. "Ready to apologize?"

"If you are."

"All right, all right! You know exactly the wrong thing to say, don't you? You know how we feel about the Turks."

"I've a cousin married to an Armenian; I ought to know. Now why couldn't I have told Dugan all this in my apartment?"

He shrugged. He started to say something and Preston, a uniformed officer, came in.

Preston took my statement while Captain Apoyan went out to give the vultures of the press some tidbits. He came in again before we were finished.

Preston finished and went out. I stood up.

Captain Apoyan said, "Turn to the right when you go out, if you want to miss the reporters. Unless you need the publicity."

"I don't. Anything else, Captain?"

"Yes," he said. "Mrs. Galbini asked me for the name of a first-rate investigator. I gave her your name."

"Well, thank you! And why does she need one?"

"I have no idea. Unless she distrusts the Department efficiency or honesty. That couldn't be possible, could it?"

"It's possible," I admitted, "but unfair. Los Angeles has one of the finest Police Departments in the country, hasn't it?"

"You tell me," he said. "Has it?"

"Yes," I said. "Good night, Captain."

"Good night, Joe," he said. "Thanks for dropping down."

He was a cutie, that Apoyan. I went out and turned to the right, down a corridor that led to a back door. Another uniformed man was waiting on the parking lot there to take me home.

I was in bed again before four-thirty and slept until nine.

The murder had happened too late last night for my edition of the Los Angeles *Times;* the murderer had made a serious mistake in alienating the *Times* right from the start. I read the sport pages with my humble breakfast.

I finished my fifth egg at the same time as the account of last night's fistic fiasco. The writer hadn't thought much of the fight and even less of Terry Lopez. I had a feeling he didn't rate Hans Mueller too highly, either, but that was an inference of mine and not stated in the article.

In the groggy hours of my awakening last night, I had neglected to ask Captain Apoyan who had steered him onto me and if they had any other reason to assume the fight was crooked.

It hadn't looked crooked; it had looked like the triumph of conditioning over loose living. Perhaps, if Mrs. Galbini came in to see me this morning, she could enlighten me.

She came into the office around eleven, a stocky straw-

blonde with a hard though attractive face. She appeared to
be about twenty years younger than her late husband.

She sat in my customer's chair calmly, with no evidence
of recent mourning. She said, "Captain Apoyan recommended
you."

"I know, Mrs. Galbini. He told me he had, last night.
What puzzled me was Captain Apoyan's assumption the fight
was fixed. Where could he have picked that up?"

"Gus bet on Mueller," she said flatly, "and the police found
out about it."

I said nothing, startled.

"Maybe it was illegal," she said. "Any bet on a fight is illegal. But it wasn't crooked. Gus rode with that bedroom
battler too damned long. Lopez cost Gus plenty of money
and gave him plenty of grief. And Gus knew he was no match
for the German. He figured he had a few dollars coming out
of the bastard."

I still said nothing, staring at this poised and realistic
widow without weeds.

Her smile was brief and cool. "You think I should be in
mourning?"

I shrugged.

"We weren't that close," she explained. "Gus took me out
of a—well, out of a career that leads nowhere. I kept his house
for him and he wasn't tight with me. I didn't ask him any
questions and he didn't make any demands. This much,
though, I owe him. This, and the cremation." She paused.
"And there'll still be a few dollars left."

I tried to think of something to say but found nothing.

"What do you charge?" she asked me.

"A hundred a day, and expenses. It's fair to warn you,
though, that the police are better equipped and charge
nothing."

"They'll be working on it anyway," she said. "And you'll
probably run across some people who'd open up to you but
not to the law." She looked at me critically. "Especially
women."

"Thank you," I said archly. "Let's be frank—is it possible
Gus could have been killed by a betrayed husband?"

"I doubt it," she said. "He didn't mess much with married
women. A betrayed boy friend now—maybe." She nodded.
"Or somebody who bet on Lopez, bet heavy."

"Do you know anybody like that?"

"No," she said slowly, "but I know the man who handled
Gus's bet." She paused. "Al Martino."

The name was only dimly familiar to me. But it brought

up the memory of another, Salvadore Peter Martino, alias Bugsy Martin, deceased.

I asked, "Any relation to Bugsy Martin?"

She nodded, "A brother. Why?"

"It makes it all so warm and together-ish," I said. "Gus introduced Terry to his wife, Terry's sister to Bugsy and now Bugsy's brother spreads the money that Gus is going to win off the defeat of Bugsy's girl friend's brother. A real compact case, should be a cinch—to get nowhere."

"At a hundred a day," she asked, "did you expect it to be easy?"

"No ma'am," I said humbly. "Anything else you can tell me that might help?"

She shook her head.

I asked, "Any idea where I might find Al Martino?"

"None. You could look under rocks."

"Well, I'll get right to work."

"Fine," she said. "How do you operate, with daily reports?"

I nodded. "Every day, neatly typed and mailed before I go home." I smiled. "Fair enough?"

She smiled back, brazenly. "You could drop over and save the typing."

In bad taste, I thought. Her husband not even ashes, yet. But I smiled and said, "That would be ten cents extra, for gas."

She stood up and her face was blank once more. "I didn't mean to be pushy. Carry on." She nodded a goodbye and went out.

I was embarrassed. I had rebuffed her. She was a lot of woman and undoubtedly worth while and I had acted oafishly. Not out of any decent instincts, but only because I liked skinny girls.

As I told her, this case was all knotted up with family ties, so the logical first choice for questioning would be one of that cozy group. My urge was to head back for the Cheviot Hills domicile of Mary Loper.

Instead, I headed for Olympic Boulevard.

The bald, short, and usually jovial Barney Delamater was again in the corner office of his immense gym. He didn't look too happy this morning, though.

He had a later edition of the *Times* on his desk. He looked up as I entered and tapped the paper. "Terrible thing," he said.

I nodded and sat down in a chair near one of his files. "Remember last time I was in here?"

He nodded. "So?"

"And after I left, Gus came in. And you two talked so earnestly about something——"

"Hey," he interrupted, scowling, "wait a minute! Who the hell do you think you are——Dick Tracy?"

"I'm better than Tracy," I told him. "I'm bigger and I'm a little smarter. What did you two talk about, Barney?"

"About the weather," he said. "How do I remember what we talked about? We sure as hell didn't talk about knocking him off. What's the pitch?"

"I know, and the police know, that Gus Galbini bet on Mueller. That would indicate the fight was fixed, wouldn't it?"

Barney shook his head. "That would indicate Gus had eyes. Though it was a damn fool thing to do."

A silence while we stared at each other. Finally, I said, "Barney, nothing happens in or around a boxing ring in this town that you don't know about. I've been hired to find Gus Galbini's murderer."

"Good luck," he said. His face showed nothing.

We stared some more. This wasn't the genial extrovert of my last visit; this was a man clamming up.

"Scared?" I asked him.

"Of what?"

"I don't know. You tell me."

"I'm a businessman," he said. "I've got a health studio that's keeping me fat. Because I'm a sucker, I've also got this gym where the stumblebums can give each other lumps. I grew up in boxing and it was always full of mugs. But I never used to be scared, because the hoodlums weren't organized in the old days. They didn't own the towns and the labor unions and most of the entertainment racket. Why shouldn't I be scared? Congress is."

"I'm not," I said.

"You're too damned stupid to be scared," he answered. "Joe, I don't know who killed Gus Galbini. And I'll tell you something else——*I don't want to know.*"

"You don't want to tell me anything, do you?"

He shrugged. "I'll talk about horses, if you want. Baseball? The weather?"

I stood up. "Thanks a *lot!* I hope you're not next, Barney."

"So do I," he said. "I'm expanding that health studio. I'm tearing out those rings and putting in bust developers. To hell with boxing and boxers; I've had it."

"Horse manure," I said. "You've been saying that for years."

"I know it," he said, "but I never sent out for reconstruction bids, before. So long, Joe. Don't hurry back."

"So long," I said. "I'll dance on your grave."

I left him with that thought and went out, fuming.

It was lunchtime now and I was hungry. At a drive-in, while I ate and admired the girls in their tight pants, I thought back to the gym and the frightened Barney 'Delamater.

His fear hadn't necessarily meant he knew anything of value to my investigation. There are always rumors floating around the fight game and 90 per cent of them are nonsense. Barney may have heard a few and put together an entirely erroneous picture in his mind. That was a possibility.

There was still the possibility, though, that he did know something. He had always been solvent, a rarity in the business, and a number of managers and fighters had reason to feel indebted to him. And a number of gamblers.

Perhaps, later, Barney would loosen up a little. He had never been known as a gutless man.

From the drive-in, I went to the triplex on the fringe of Cheviot Hills. But there was one of those cardboard "will return" clocks on the door of Mary Loper and the hands informed me her expected hour of return would be six o'clock.

I had hoped she would be able to give me the address of Al Martino. Her absence sent me west, toward her brother's wife. Weird case. . . .

Bridget Gallegher Lopez was in shorts and T-shirt and her lightly freckled face didn't brighten at the sight of me. She stood in the doorway and asked, "Now, what?"

"Now Galbini's dead," I answered, "and I have a new client and I'm sure you want to cooperate if it will help to find a killer."

"I don't know anything," she said. "And if I did, I'd rather not talk with you about it."

"We started off as such great friends," I told her sadly. "Why are you so difficult, Mrs. Lopez?"

"You'd better go," she said, "if you know what's good for you. My husband is resting and he can get nasty if he's disturbed."

I smiled at her. "Bridget, he's only a middleweight. I could crush him easily in either hand."

She glared at me and started to close the door.

I said quickly, "You're involved, you know. The police know you hired me to investigate Galbini. They questioned me about it."

She was quiet for a moment, still staring, and then she said, "Come in, but keep your voice down."

In the paneled living room, she said softly, "I couldn't be involved. Do the police think Terry is?"

"Because of the bet, do you mean, the bet Gus made on Mueller?"

I scored with that. Her eyes widened with surprise and she said quickly, "That wasn't in the paper."

"I know a lot of things that aren't in the paper, Mrs. Lopez. We both do, don't we?"

She said nothing, looking uncertain.

"Your husband has a reputation for being hot-tempered," I went on. "I'm sure he resented learning that Gus bet on Mueller. I suppose he's been questioned all morning."

"He was questioned for an hour," she said. "And so was I." Her chin went up. "And so was the high fashion model, Mary Loper." Her eyes narrowed. "Are you working for her?"

I shook my head. "Is there anything you want to tell me that you didn't tell the police?"

"I told them everything," she said. "How about you?"

"I told them all I had to, to keep my license. Then one of the—principals in the case asked Captain Apoyan at the West Side Station to recommend a private investigator and he recommended me." I smiled. "And here I am, back on the merry-go-round."

"One of the principals? Which one?"

I said nothing.

She asked, "Why tell me that the police recommended you? Are you trying to impress me, or—to blackmail us?" Her voice was shrill.

"You know better than that. You're getting hysterical, Mrs. Lopez. I'd better go."

And then from my right, a voice said, "That's right. And quick!"

I turned to see Terry Lopez standing there in the archway that led to the dining room. After his beating of last night, I was surprised he could stand.

"I'm on the way," I told him, and really was.

But the bigmouth had to add, "Unless you'd like me to belt you."

I turned back and smiled. "You couldn't walk this far. And if you could, the Queensbury rules wouldn't prevail. Don't press your hundred-and-sixty-pound luck."

He returned my smile. "I can walk that far." He came over slowly to stand in front of me.

The hair began to bristle on my neck and I started to caution him once more, but never made it.

I didn't see the punch—that's my excuse. It came from nowhere and landed cleanly on the jaw. The shock was bearable, the pain minimal. What really flooded through me was shame.

I went down into the black pit knowing I'd been kayoed by a lousy, stinking middleweight. . . .

chapter four

WHEN I CAME TO, ON THE LIVING ROOM CARPETING, HE wasn't in sight. Mrs. Lopez was bathing my face with a wet towel.

"Where is he?" I mumbled. "Where's the bastard hiding? This one didn't count." I pushed the towel aside.

She put a hand on my shoulder and pressed me down again. "Relax," she said. "He went out. I warned you, Mr. Puma."

"He could be in trouble," I told her. "A fighter's fists are considered a lethal weapon in California. He could be in a lot of trouble."

"Protecting his home?" she asked me. "After you forced your way in here?"

I stared at her. "That's a lie."

She smiled. "And I'm the girl who can put it over. Get up slowly, now; your eyes are still glazed."

I got up slowly, my knees weak. I stood up and tried not to sway and fingered my sore jaw. "Pretty good punch," I admitted, "for a man with nothing else."

Fire in the bright eyes, rigidity in the fine body.

"You love him," I said. "I'm sorry for you."

"Sit down," she said. "You're still weak; you're trembling."

"With anger," I said. "I'm not weak. I'll meet him again. Maybe I can put him into the gas chamber."

A senseless, adolescent, loser's remark. But, for some reason, it scored.

Her bright eyes searched my face and there was a subtle apprehension in the air around us. She whispered, "What are you talking about?"

"About Terry Lopez," I said. "Who else?"

There was no conviction in her voice. "You're talking non-

sense. The police know where he was when Gus was killed.
I told them. He was with me, at home, in bed."

I gave her my knowing look #2A. "Sure he was. I'm not
the police, Mrs. Lopez. I have informants who wouldn't
think of ever going to the police with *anything.*" I added
a little coal. "And Al Martino has friends who can't afford
to even be seen by the police." Which was no lie. Meaningless, but no lie.

"Al Martino?" she asked hoarsely. "Bugsy's brother?"

"He handled the money. He found the suckers for Gus."
Her eyes continued to search my face.

"It's amazing, isn't it," I commented, "how many things
don't find their way into the newspapers?" I stretched my
neck and rubbed my jaw. "Well, I'd better get along. There
must be a few people more cooperative than you've been.
Thanks for nothing."

"Wait," she said. She looked past me, her eyes fearful
and thoughtful. She looked at me. "Sit down. There's no
hurry. He won't be back for a while."

I sat down near the sliding glass door through which I
could view the Village of Westwood.

She sat near-by and stared thoughtfully at the carpeting.
"Terry's no killer," she said quietly.

"He certainly didn't look like one last night," I agreed.

She flushed faintly. "He has an unreasonable temper. But
I know he couldn't—cold-bloodedly kill someone."

She was building up to something; I waited.

"Don't you believe that?" she asked me. "You have to
believe that."

"I don't know him well enough to believe anything," I
answered.

A silence. In the village, far below, I could see the cars
move with the traffic lights, clogging, unclogging, flowing,
stopping.

An intake of breath, and she said softly, "He wasn't with
me when Gus was killed."

I kept my face bland, like a good liar. "Is that supposed
to be news?"

"I thought you knew," she said. "I thought that's why you
came here. How did you find it out?"

I didn't answer, staring at her.

"And now you'll tell the police?" she asked.

"Have I, up to now?"

"Why haven't you?" she asked.

To myself, I said, *because I didn't know it.* To her, I
said, "Where did he tell you he was?"

"Out, alone, walking around, that's what he told me. He probably wasn't. He was probably with some—woman."

"Maybe," I said, looking enigmatic.

Her voice rose. "Do you know he wasn't? Why can't you tell me what you know?"

"Because I'm not working for you any longer, Mrs. Lopez. And while we're on that subject, why did you fire me?"

She looked at her carpeting again. It was fine carpeting. "Because of your—insolence. About the bill, I—received it. I could pay it right now, if you want."

"I'm in no hurry," I said. "It isn't really due until the first of next month."

She chewed her lower lip. "I could pay—a little extra. I actually contracted to hire you for longer than—"

I raised a hand. "I'm not a blackmailer, Mrs. Lopez. I've been hired by a client to work with the police in finding the murderer of Gus Galbini. I'm not a scandalmonger or a keyhole-peeper and I sell nothing but my investigative service. You've got the wrong slant on me." I paused. "From somebody."

"Then why didn't you tell the police about Terry not being home last night?" she asked.

The impulse to be honest was strong. But the impulse to find a killer was stronger. "I've explained that. I'm not in the scandal business."

"Then he was with a woman?"

"Don't you know?"

She shook her head slowly.

"Tell me about Gus and why you had me investigate him."

"Because I heard what the police know now, that Gus was betting on Mueller. Honestly, that's the whole reason."

"And where did you hear that?"

"From Terry," she said. "I don't know where he heard it."

"And that's all you have to tell me?"

She nodded. "But haven't you something to tell me?"

"Nothing you should know, Mrs. Lopez. I swear it. I have no idea if your husband was with a woman last night, or not." I stood up. "The fact that you lied about his being with you last night is something I won't tell the police right now."

"Right now?"

"Never, unless it's concerned with the murder."

"It isn't," she said. "I know it isn't. I'll mail you that check tomorrow."

I thanked her in advance and left. I had tricked her into an admission and I wasn't proud of my tactics, but how else could I function? Double talk and luck, those were my weapons. And my sturdy Latin intuition.

Sergeant Marty Dugan wasn't working this afternoon, nor Apoyan. But another detective sergeant gave me what they had at the Purdue Street Station.

The apartment where Gus had been shot last night was in a building he owned, an apartment house of six one-bedroom units. It was a furnished apartment and so far as the Department had been able to learn, had never been rented.

"Love nest, maybe?" the sergeant said. "Would he need it? Hell, he was at least fifty." He shuffled through some papers. "Fifty-one."

He was young for a sergeant. I smiled. "Maybe he used it for poker."

"Then why that king-sized bed?"

I shrugged and riffled through the statements of the principals and the occupants of neighboring apartments in Gus's building. They were all carbons.

"The originals have been sent downtown," the sergeant told me. "It will be handled from there, of course."

"How about Sergeant Dugan?"

"He'll work on it. And Captain Apoyan will help. He used to be in Homicide, before he was sent out here."

I nodded and continued to read the reports. Two of the tenants in the building had heard the report of a gun at about two o'clock; it had been loud enough to get them out of bed and prompt one to phone the police.

Nobody had seen the killer. One tenant, who had not heard the shot, had earlier seen an unfamiliar car in the neighborhood, a gray Bentley sedan.

I read through the rest of it and told the sergeant, "I guess Gus didn't use the place for poker, after all."

"How come you figure that?"

I showed him the inventory sheet. "Five bottles of cologne up there and not a single deck of cards."

The sergeant shook his head wonderingly. "Fifty-one years old— He probably played spin-the-bottle."

I left him lost in wonder and went out into a dying day. I thought of the cardboard clock on the door of Mary Loper and steered the Plymouth toward Cheviot Hills.

It was only five-thirty when I got there; she wasn't home. I sat on her red brick patio.

It wasn't long before I heard the grate of a footstep on concrete and looked up to see Mary Loper coming along the sidewalk that led to the alley. She had a bag of groceries in one arm.

I watched her approach, slim and fairly tall, with a chin-high, erect, model's walk, dressed in the chic copy of a much more expensive Irish linen suit.

"You?" she said. "Who asked for you?" She stopped walking and stared at me without rancor. "And at dinnertime, too."

"I didn't come for dinner," I told her. "I came for an address."

"Whose?"

"Al Martino's."

A pause, and then, "I don't know it."

"Have you seen him lately?"

"This morning," she said. "He was waiting for me when I left the police station. I was questioned this morning."

"Will you be seeing him again?"

"I hope not." Her face was grave. "Will I?"

I shrugged.

We stood there silently for a few seconds, and then she said, "Will you take the key out of my purse and open the door?"

The purse was under her arm. I took the key out and opened the door and stood aside for her to enter. She went into the kitchen, and I didn't follow.

In a second, she asked, "Aren't you coming in?"

I came in and stood near the doorway. She put her groceries down and turned to me. "There's enough steak. I've had a good week and I bought extra steak for the freezer."

"I wouldn't think of imposing," I protested.

"Like hell you wouldn't," she said mildly. "I wish you'd stay. I'm—frightened."

"It's about time," I told her. "Are you going to broil the steaks outside?"

"I'm no good with charcoal," she said. "I can't seem to get it glowing right."

"I'm good at it," I said.

"The paper and the kindling are out there," she told me. "I'll mix us a drink in the meanwhile. Martini okay?"

"On the rocks," I told her, and went out to the patio.

I had the charcoal started when she brought my drink out. She had taken off the jacket to the suit and thrown a cashmere sweater over her shoulders.

We sat on the chaise longues and she asked, "What did you mean when you said it was about time I was frightened?"

"I shouldn't have said it," I answered. "I'm too—mouthy."

"You meant I should have been frightened all the time I was a friend of Sal's, didn't you?"

"I guess." I sipped my drink. Too much vermouth.

"He never gave me reason to be frightened," she said evenly. "Not *once*."

"And who has given you reason now?"

"The murder." She took a breath. "And then Al waiting for me— I never liked him. He's not at all like Sal."

"What did he want this morning?"

"He wanted to know what the police had asked me. He wanted to know if they knew the fight had been fixed, if they'd said anything like that. I told him they hadn't." She stared at me. "Was it crooked?"

I hesitated and said, "There's a strong rumor around that Gus Galbini bet on Mueller." I paused. "And that Al Martino handled the bet."

"Gus?" She shook her head. "Does Terry know Gus bet on Mueller?"

"So I've heard. But Terry's covered for the time that Gus was killed. His wife is his alibi."

"Terry?" she said, startled. "Surely the police can't think of Terry as a murderer?"

"With his temper?"

"But a gun?" she said. "I can see him hitting someone in anger, but not using a gun. Oh, no—that's impossible."

I said nothing.

"Are you working with the police?" she asked me. "You're not a policeman, are you?"

"I'm working with the police," I said. "But for a client. For Mrs. Gus Galbini. She's not my original client."

Silence. In the west, the sun was turning the clouds pink and the mountains purple. On the lee side of the ridges, the foothills were black.

For minutes, neither of us said a word.

Then she asked, "How do you like your steak?"

"Practically raw."

"I'll put mine on now," she said. "I like it well done."

She put one on and came back to sip her drink again. "Quiet, aren't we?"

"I'm relaxing. I'm—recovering." I told her about Terry's lucky punch.

"It isn't the first time," she said. "That sort of thing he's done since he was twelve. But a gun? Never, never, *never*—"

She could be wrong, even if it was her brother. She had been way wrong on Bugsy Martin. I withheld comment.

Another few minutes of peace and she set her drink on a low table near-by and said, "We should have a salad, too." She rose and went into the kitchen.

There was a tension in the air.

Sex, some call it. Ultimate communication is closer to the truth. Supreme ecstacy? Put it down as a drive second only to self-preservation, a drive that has put men into outer space eons before the birth of the rocket.

Was it a personal awareness, limited to one? My practiced intuition told me it was shared. Had I invited myself to dinner? And Bugsy Martin had been dead a long time. She was human.

She came out again and asked, "What are you thinking about?"

"Salvadore Peter Martino," I answered.

"Bugsy?" she said lightly. "He's dead."

In the wind, a straw, a pretty big straw. "Anything I can do to help?" I asked.

"Just sit there," she said, "calm, strong, and personable. You have no idea how comforting your presence is."

She bent over to turn her steak, and I thought I noticed tension in the movement. In the hills, the purple had blended with the black, but the pink and white clouds still rode the rim of the horizon. The smell of steak and charcoal and burning fat drifted down my way.

She sat down again and sipped her drink and we talked and later we ate. The sun went down; we went into the house. We were friends by this time; we had mutual friends.

The aura of awareness was mutual now, I felt sure. All I needed was a trigger.

It happened in the kitchen. I was putting glasses away and she was right next to me, putting the clean silverware in a drawer. I turned away from the cupboard as she turned away from the drawer, and there we were, face to face.

And she looked up, smiling, and her chin lifted and her voice was a little hoarse. "Hello," she said.

And I pulled her close; there was no resistance. She came eagerly, her lips open, her body pressing fiercely.

chapter five

ON THE LOW WIDE BED SHE LAY QUIETLY, STARING OUT THE window at the yellow moon. I lay basked in remembrance of her wiry agility, her soaring cooperation, her murmurs, and her kisses.

Her brown, taut body was outlined in the moonlight, her brown hair was awry on the pillow.

"It's been a long time," she said, without looking at me. "I hope I didn't startle you."

I said nothing.

"Were you ever married?" she asked.

"Never. Were you?"

She sighed. "Never. Do you think it would stay this way, wild and wonderful, after the wedding?"

"For a year, maybe. Six months. I don't know. With all the infidelity in the world, something must be wrong with marriage."

"Maybe it's just that there's something wrong with people." She turned over to face me. "You're gentle for a man so big."

Wasn't Bugsy? I thought, but said only, "Thank you."

She inhaled audibly, and said again in a whisper, "It's been a long time."

Again, I said nothing.

Until she added, "Am I crowding you? Am I a glutton?"

It wasn't until then I realized what she meant by a long time. "You're not crowding me," I said. "Two glasses of milk, and I'll be a new man."

I wasn't new but I was adequate, which was quite an accomplishment considering it hadn't been a long time for me. And there had been only a glass and a half of milk in the refrigerator.

37

At three o'clock, a sound pulled me to consciousness and I listened carefully but heard nothing. Until just as I was falling back to sleep again, I heard her murmur, "Bugsy, Bugsy, Bugsy——"

In the morning when I wakened she was gone. She had left a note on the drainboard in the kitchen:

> "Gentle One:
> "An early appointment and you looked too peaceful to disturb. There is plenty of food——make your own damned breakfast!
>
> "Mary"

There was certainly plenty of food. Her refrigerator was a two-door monster and it was crammed. A psychiatrist could probably find some symbolism there.

The eggs were extra large and the bacon a premium brand. The coffee percolator was more than half full. I fed my depleted strength and then phoned my answering service.

I was informed that a Mr. Snip Caster had phoned and would expect a return call.

I went out to the Plymouth and saw the Department car parked across the street. There was no one in it. I waited for a few seconds, wondering if they were looking for me, but nobody appeared. I climbed into my car and headed for Venice.

Snip was outside again, on the gray lawn getting the sun. "A little while ago," he said, "you were here asking about Gus Galbini. And now he's dead, huh?"

"That's right. Don't be cryptic. If you have something to tell me, spill it."

"Why *tell* it," he asked, "when I can *sell* it?"

I shook my head. "I happen to be a poor man."

"So you're poor," he said. "The people you usually work for aren't poor. And I'll bet you're working on the Galbini kill."

I nodded.

"For some rich guy," he added.

"No. But maybe my client would stand still for a little padding on the expense account. That is, if you've got anything I can use."

"You can use it," he said. "It's about Mueller and somebody else."

Hans Mueller. . . . I'd never thought of this case from *his*

angle. I asked, "Is it important? Do you think what you
know would help me?"

He nodded.

"I think," I said, "my client will stand still for a twenty-
five-buck item on the swindle sheet. I can't go any higher
than that, Snip."

He was silent, thinking. He was probably translating the
dollars into terms he understood, pints and fifths and quarts.
Finally, he said, "There was a meeting three nights ago in
Barney Delamater's office. Around midnight. Mueller, Doc
Golde, Barney, Galbini, and Al Martino. How's that for a
combination? And midnight, yet!"

"Who's Doc Golde?" I asked.

"Mueller's manager, his brain, his financial noodle."

"Some combination," I agreed, "and what could it mean?"

"One thing I heard it meant is that Galbini got a piece of
Mueller. Did the police find anything that makes that true?"

"If they did, they didn't confide in me." I opened my wallet.
Luckily, it was fatter than usual. I gave Snip two tens and a
five and asked, "Anything more you know about the meeting?"

He shook his head. He folded the bills quickly and shoved
them into the pocket of his shorts, glancing once more at the
house.

"Keep your ears open," I said. I held up the wallet. "It's
not empty yet."

"Big wheel," he said scornfully. "I used to pay twenty-
five bucks for a dinner."

Used to— Used to— The town was full of used-to-be's. I
headed right for the West Side Station.

Sergeant Dugan was out working, but Captain Apoyan was
in. I gave him the information I'd just received from Snip.

"Who told you this?" he asked me.

I shook my head and said nothing.

He frowned, annoyed. Then he ticked them off on his
fingers; "Delamater, Golde, Mueller, Galbini." He paused.
"And Al Martino. Have you run across him yet?"

"No. Has the Department?"

He shook his head. "And we had good reason to believe
he's involved."

"I heard he handled the bet for Galbini."

Apoyan looked even more annoyed. "You hear a lot, don't
you? How come we don't hear it from you?"

"You just did, Captain. But I'd like to ask you why you
didn't tell me Galbini had bet on Mueller? You could have

told me that the night Sergeant Dugan dragged me down here."

"We're not obligated to tell you anything," he said coldly.

His annoyance must have been contagious. Because I had it, now. I sat there glaring at him.

He returned the glare for a few seconds and then something close to a smile warmed his broad face. "A paisan and a purple-foot," he said. "I guess we're too much alike to get along, aren't we?"

"I need you," I said frankly. "But I think you need me, too. I play it a little cuter than the Department man, but you can call any number of officers downtown I've worked with successfully."

"I already have," he said. "Okay, Joe; you work your way and we'll work our way. *Together*. Now, the way I see it, you're the man to check into this summit meeting in Delamater's gym."

"Why?"

"Because none of them are men who are impressed by the law, except maybe Mueller. The chances are they might confide a few things to you. But nothing, I'm sure, to us."

He had a point. My only quest was for a murderer. The police were almost obligated to pick up principals in a case who were guilty of something less than the murder. I wasn't.

"Okay," I agreed. And asked, "You got a file on Martino here?"

"I just phoned downtown," he said. "I'll have it soon."

I hesitated and then said, "He was right outside here, in front of your station, yesterday morning."

Apoyan looked started. "Who told you that?"

I hesitated once more, and then said, "He was waiting for somebody you were questioning—Mary Loper."

"Oh?" Then he smiled. "Did she tell you that last night?"

I stared at him.

He continued to smile. "You ought to know her pretty well by now."

I thought of the Department car I had seen in front of her place. I said quietly, "Am I under suspicion, too, Captain?"

"Of course not, Joe," he said with false geniality. "We only want to protect you. Think of us as your watchful father."

"I don't need ten thousand fathers," I told him. "I'm a big boy now."

"You sure as hell are," he admitted, and waved a dismissal. "Go see Delamater and the others."

There was no room to park on the street near Barney's; I turned off Olympic and went around the corner to his parking lot. One of the doors near his office opened onto this lot.

There were about fifteen cars on this lot but only one of special significance. Right next to the double door leading into the gym, a gray Bentley sedan was parked.

I walked over to check the registration slip strapped to the steering shaft housing. Business must be good; the car was Barney's.

I went past the door that led to the health studio and through the double door that led to the gym. There were no signs of reconstruction work in progress.

In his office, Barney said, "You again?" He didn't smile.

"The police been here?" I asked.

"Not today. Why?"

"That car of yours out on the lot—that's the kind that was parked near the apartment where Gus was killed."

"That's not only the kind, that's the car," he admitted. "But it was gone long before Gus ever got there."

"How do you know when Gus got there?"

"I don't," he said, "but I know it was after the fight. And the poker game I was playing in broke up before the fight. Most of us went to the fight."

"Was Gus in the game?"

He snorted. "Before a big fight? Of course not!"

"Who was?"

"None of your damned business."

"Al Martino, maybe?"

His eyes were blank. "Who's he?"

"You know who he is. He was here, at midnight, three nights ago. He was here and so were you. And so were Galbini, Mueller, and Doc Golde."

Barney was motionless in his chair. His breathing seemed heavier. He said nothing.

"Barney," I said agreeably, "we used to be sort of half-assed friends. When did you get the idea you couldn't trust me?"

"When you got on my back and into my business. You can't prove that, about that gang being here. And what if they were?"

"It should make interesting news to the Boxing Commission. Especially with Al Martino here. And a *midnight* meeting. What was it, a seance?"

"Maybe it was a meeting of the Joe Puma Fan Club," he answered hoarsely. "And maybe there wasn't any meeting at all. Funny the cops didn't ask me about that. Or is this some *private* information you got?"

"That's the way I work, privately." I took a breath. "Do you want me to go? Or have you decided to become a citizen?"

For a second, I thought I saw indecision on his face. But he said, "You can go any time. Why don't you bother the others, if you think they were here? Why don't you ask Al Martino if he was here?"

"As soon as he comes out of hiding, I intend to ask him."

Barney smiled coldly. "I'll bet. Who the hell do you think he's hiding from—*you?*"

"Probably not. But when you see him, you tell him I'm looking for him. My office and my home addresses are in the phone book."

He looked at his desk top. He looked up and his face was softer. "Joe, your size gives you some strange ideas. Get smart and don't tangle with Al Martino."

"I don't take advice from the gutless, Barney," I told him. "I'll leave now and you can crawl back into your hole." I started for the door.

"Joe—" he called, and I turned.

"I'm telling you as a friend," he said quietly, "as a former, half-assed friend—Vegas is getting stronger in this town every day. Don't mess with those boys. They've got national tie-ups."

"So have we, Barney," I said. "One's the Declaration of Independence and the other is the Constitution. And you tell Al I'm taking full advantage of the Second Amendment."

He frowned. "What's that about?"

"About the right of the people to keep and bear arms. You tell that two-bit hoodlum my arm is a .38 and I know which end to point."

"Oh God," he said, "dear God—"

It was more prayer than curse and he was right, of course.

I was in one hell of a mood and it didn't improve. Because, after lunch, I spent one of the most frustrating afternoons of my life.

At the hotel where Mueller and Golde were staying, I was told that Mueller was in Palm Springs for a few days, but Doc Golde could be reached at his broker's office. It wasn't far; I drove over.

He had just left, a girl there told me, but could be found at a bar only a block and a half away. I arrived at the bar in time to learn that Golde had consumed one drink, found no gin rummy players present and gone on to a bar farther downtown.

Enough of that; I never did catch up with him.

From downtown to the Lopez residence above Westwood is a long trip and heavily trafficked. But maybe, if I got them together, and they could be convinced of the discretion of my investigation, I could learn more than either was likely to tell me alone.

I didn't get them together or separately. Nobody was home.

Barney uncooperative, Galbini dead, Mueller in Palm Springs, Doc Golde elusive, Martino not to be found—where next?

Perhaps, with the new knowledge I had picked up on her late husband, Mrs. Galbini could fill in some gaps. I drove over there.

You guessed it; she wasn't home.

I drove back to the office to type up the report of this fruitless, maddening day. The same pink clouds filled the Western sky as last evening's; the hills were just as beautiful.

But my mood was murderous.

In my office, I typed it up, hunt and peck, listening to the sound of Doctor Dale Graves's drill next door and smelling the carbon monoxide that came through the open window from the street below.

I have a pretty fair twenty-four-hour memory and I managed an almost verbatim transcript of the dialogues. All my conversation with Mary Loper that could be construed as investigation I included but nothing about where I had spent the night. There was no point in making Mrs. Galbini jealous.

I finished, making two carbon copies, one for Apoyan. I sat there, waiting for the sound of Dr. Graves's drill to stop, sulking and moody.

I heard footsteps in the hall outside and hoped that, if it was another Graves's patient, he'd need extraction and not drilling. It wasn't a Graves's patient; it was a Puma visitor.

Palm Springs tan and Sunset Strip tailoring. Manicured nails, bench-made shoes, glossy black hair, and confident smile. About a hundred and ninety pounds of contemporary hoodlum.

"My name," he said, "is Al Martino and I understand you've been looking for me."

"I sure as hell have," I told him. "Sit down."

He stood a few feet from the far side of the desk, still smiling. "I'm comfortable the way I am, thank you. What did you want?"

The faint odor of his cologne drifted over. I said, "I want the answers to some questions."

His beautifully lashed brown eyes surveyed me sleepily. "And who the hell are you to ask *me* questions?"

"I'm a citizen, Martino," I explained, "a citizen licensed by the state to ask questions. One of the questions concerns a meeting you and some others attended in Barney Delamater's gym a few midnights ago."

"Who told you about that?" he asked.

"It doesn't matter. I—"

He held up a hand. "I asked you a question, peeper."

The redness in my mind. I kept my voice low. "I answered it. I'll ask the questions."

Wonder in his voice. "I heard about you, but I didn't believe it. Paisan, you've got to be kidding. Even a moron like you must realize I'm not bush league."

"Would you get downwind from me?" I asked him. "Your perfume is making me excited."

Color in his face and then it drained. He stood like a statue. Adrenalin moved into my blood stream as I held his glare.

He said, "Some guys won't learn the bright way, will they?" His hand started to move.

I said, "If you're going for a gun, don't. Because there's a .38 in my hand, complete with hollow point bullets. It's aimed at your belly."

There wasn't any gun in my hand, but my hands were below the top of the desk and his body was in line with the kneehole in the desk.

"I don't carry a gun," he said. "I'm big enough so I don't need to carry a gun."

I put my empty hands on the desk. "Just a little bluff. Scared you, though, didn't it?"

He shook his head. "Listen carefully. You've already learned too damned much. Forget what you've learned. I suppose you think that little tramp Sal used to shack with can give you the picture on me. Both of you are on damned thin ice and—"

I stood up. I came around the desk and put a hand on his shoulder. "What little tramp?"

He tensed, but his voice was calm. "That Loper broad."

I tightened the grip of my left hand on his shoulder and threw the right hand into his belly. He jackknifed, grunting sickly, and went down to both knees on the floor.

He managed to whisper, "You won't live twenty-four hours, now."

I shifted my left-hand grip to his throat and pulled him to his feet. I backhanded him, and said, "You didn't mean 'tramp,' did you? It was a slip of the tongue."

"Twenty-four hours," he repeated.

I tightened my grip on his throat, and he clawed at me, choking and whimpering. I dragged him over to the desk and picked up the phone. I asked the operator downstairs to get me the West Side Station as Martino's knees began to sag and his struggling grew weaker.

I reached Apoyan and told him, "I'm holding Al Martino in my office for you. You can pick him up or maybe they'd send a man over from Headquarters here."

Headquarters here was Beverly Hills, a separate municipality, surrounded by L.A.

Apoyan said, "Hang on, Puma. Somebody will come damned quick."

Martino was limp, now. I dropped him and went over to get a pitcher of water to throw in his face.

chapter six

It was a Catholic hospital and the sister at the desk in the lobby told me softly that Captain Apoyan was in the small room visible to my right.

Apoyan was in there alone. He asked, "Who do you think you are, the Avenger? What happened?"

"I hit him in the belly," I answered. "That shouldn't put him into the hospital."

"It should if he had ulcers," Apoyan said. "And he had ulcers." He paused. "And *no* gun. You're in trouble, Puma, and I'm not sure I want to go to bat for you."

I said nothing, though many words came to my mind.

"He can hardly whisper," Apoyan went on. "Did you hit him in the Adam's apple, too?"

"I held him by the throat," I said. "I was holding him for you. Jeepers, I had to hold him by *something*, didn't I?"

"Cut it out," he said. "Cut out the stinking whimsy!"

"Who's up there with him?" I asked.

"Dugan and Ellerbe. It's—wasted time. His attorney's on the way, one of the biggest in town."

"Natch. And when he gets through double-talking you, you'll be glad I got my licks in early. And as for you going to bat for me, when did you ever?"

"Easy, now," he warned me.

"Easy, hell! You give me enough rope so I can stir up some action and get the rats out of hiding. And then when I've accomplished what you hoped I would, your cunning Armenian mind goes to work and you start playing politics."

"A bigot, too, eh?" he said quietly.

"Why not? Everybody else is. Let's be honest with each other, just for ten seconds. Captain, I don't give a damn if you go to bat for me or not. Your batting average doesn't

46

impress me. I'll call Mrs. Galbini right now, from here, and tell her I don't want the case."

"Sure you will. And throw away a hundred a day? That, I want to see."

There was a phone in the room and a phone book. I looked up Mrs. Galbini's number, picked up the phone— and Apoyan said wearily, "Put it down, hothead. Nobody's impressed."

I replaced the phone in its cradle and looked at him.

"Damn you," he said. "You can't do anything with *dignity*. You can't ever operate like an officer of the law, can you?"

"No," I said. "How many officers did you have out looking for Martino?"

A moment's silence, and then a tall and dignified man came into the room, with a very impressive manner and a sonorous voice.

"Captain Apoyan?"

Apoyan nodded.

"My name is Sylvester Thornton. I'm here to represent Albert Martino."

Apoyan nodded again.

Thornton frowned, took a breath and looked at me. "Mr. Puma, I believe?"

"Right."

"You—attacked my client."

"Not really, Mr. Thornton. I tried to—I mean— Oh hell, I don't know how to say it." I put on my embarrassed face and stared moodily at the floor.

"Perhaps," he said coldly, "you'll know how to say it in court."

"I suppose," I said sadly. "Gosh, I hope there won't be any reporters around." I looked up humbly to meet his stare.

"Reporters? What are you talking about, Mr. Puma?"

"It would embarrass me, Mr. Thornton, explaining in front of all those people how Al Martino came into my office, smelling of cheap perfume, and made me an indecent proposal. And then, when I tried to repel his advances—"

"That's absurd!" he interrupted. "Are you telling me, Mr. Puma, that you're going into court and perjure yourself?"

"Why, Mr. Thornton," I said, in shock, "I would no more think of committing perjury than you would of accepting blood money from hoodlums."

Silence all around while I stared at Thornton, he at me, and Captain Apoyan at both of us.

And then I said, "You know damned well, you cheap shyster, that Al Martino wouldn't dream of taking me to court. He's got his own court, his jury, and his judge. And he's got you."

Thornton said, "You can take back that shyster remark or I'll guarantee you'll go into court."

"You can go to hell," I said.

Apoyan said, "Joe, be reasonable."

I shook my head without looking at him, holding Sylvester Thornton's glare. "I'm calling this shyster's bluff. I don't think he's ever been investigated by a first-class operator."

Thornton said to me, "You'll live to regret this." He looked at Apoyan. "May I see my client now?"

Apoyan nodded and Thornton went out.

Apoyan said, "You're absolutely crazy, 100 per cent."

"About 98 per cent," I answered. I sat on a chintz upholstered wicker love seat and lighted a cigarette. "I hate hoodlums, Captain, even when they get their law degrees at Harvard."

"Hate, hate, hate——" he said impatiently. "Is that all that ever motivates you?"

I smiled at him. "Of course not. Basically, I'm a lover. I hate the nonlovers." I sighed. "And there are so damned many of them."

"And you're a bigot," he said.

I smiled again. "Only around you. You're so sensitive about it, it brings out my worst."

"Your best is bad enough," he said. "I'd better go up and see how the boys are making out."

A pointless trip— The boys would get just exactly as many answers out of Albert Martino as they would get out of the bed he was lying in. But they had to make the effort.

Apoyan hadn't asked me to wait though he probably expected I would. Hospitals made me nervous; I went out and down the dark street to my car.

And where now? Patagonia might be a good choice as soon as Al's friends heard the bad news. Tibet, Tasmania? I headed for the home of Mrs. Gus Galbini, widow.

I was still embarrassed by my adolescent display of violence in the office. Martino had caught me at the end of a bad day and said the wrong thing. The remark about Mary Loper had been the last straw, and why should I value her virtue so highly? I couldn't rationalize it; the beast in me had won because I hated hoodlums.

My pa had always told me it was all right to hate anything but people. You should never hate people, my pa had told me, only the evil in them. And in me. He was probably right but I still hated hoodlums. I didn't think of them as people.

It was after my dinnertime and I was hungry but I continued toward my destination.

The Galbini house was on one of those wandering streets that twist back on themselves in the Riviera section of the Palisades.

Mrs. Galbini opened the door and the smell of cooking came out to make my stomach rumble.

"Close the door," I said. "The smell of that pizza is killing me."

She smiled. "Don't you like it?"

"It's my second greatest weakness."

"Come in," she said. "Come in and report and then we'll eat."

I came into a dim entry hall, through a dark living room to a brightly lighted family room in view of the open kitchen. I sat at a glass and wrought iron table in there and she brought me a can of beer and sat down across from me.

I gave her the story of my day and watched the uneasiness grow in her face and the fright come finally to her eyes.

When I had finished, she said quietly, "It's funny, but I never thought of Al Martino as a—a threat. But he must know the same people Bugsy did."

"Probably. Did you know about that midnight meeting in Delamater's gym?"

She shook her head and stood up slowly. "That pizza is about ready. Another can of beer?"

"With the pizza, please," I said. "If I had the beer first, I'd get drunk."

She smiled suddenly. as though considering the potential of a drunken Puma (a defenseless Puma?) and then went to get the pizza and more beer.

Into my cavernous stomach the pizza went, lulling the angry juices, bringing back my strength, brightening the world. It was first-class pizza.

"Are you Italian?" I asked her.

"Lithuanian," she answered. "I learned to cook all these things for Gus. He loved to eat, that man." A tear moved down her cheek.

In my office, she had been poised and adjusted; this new melancholy surprised me.

"I gave him a base," she explained. "I gave him a base to operate from and let him have his freedom and he was never cheap with me. He wasn't such a bad guy as you might be thinking."

I made no comment.

Silence for a few moments, and then she said, "That business about Terry not being home, that phony alibi his wife gave the police—are you going to tell them?"

"Not yet."

She looked at me thoughtfully. "Why not?"

"I—try to protect all the people I question unless I'm sure their secrets impede the investigation. It's just a general rule I follow in order to encourage their confidence in me."

"Especially with women?" she asked.

"With anyone," I said. "Women seem to need protection more than men."

Another period of vocal quiet while we attacked the pizza, the crisp, cold lettuce and the nutritious beer.

As she was pouring my coffee, she said, "You know who I keep thinking of? Terry Lopez. He had a juvenile police record, a real nasty one. But I suppose that's not open to investigation?"

"I might be able to get it. Violence, you mean? Gang fights?"

"He put a boy into the hospital for two months. Cut him up with a knife. Twice, he was caught with marijuana on him. Of course, that was some time ago."

"Did he and Gus quarrel much?"

"Enough." She sipped her coffee and stared at me doubtfully. "Do you think it's wise to continue the investigation, after what happened in your office?"

"It's not wise, maybe, but it's profitable. For me." I smiled at her. "I've already got Al as mad at me as he's likely to get. And I'd hate to think a puke like that could make me back down."

"I wasn't thinking of him," she said. "I was thinking of his—his friends."

"We can't be sure he has any," I argued. "Bugsy did, we know, but maybe Al's a lone wolf."

She shook her head gravely. "I doubt it."

"So do I. But I hope he is. I can't fight *everybody*." I finished my coffee. "Thanks for the meal. Could I help with the dishes?"

"I have a dishwasher, thank you. Do you—have to go?"

I met her gaze steadily and lied evenly. "I do. I have to meet a stoolie in about half an hour and it's quite a ways from here. Anything else you can tell me before I go?"

"Nothing." She looked at the tablecloth. "Good luck."

I went out feeling like a semi-heel. There had been some

invitation in her voice and I had no appointment with a stoolie. Perhaps, if last night hadn't happened. . . . I was no superman.

It was eight-thirty, too early to go home. I had learned a few things since this morning, but none of them fitted into a pattern that made any significant picture.

The moon was high and yellow, the night breeze warm. I turned onto Sunset above the golf course and rode with the traffic heading toward town.

By chance, perhaps, or maybe by subconscious design, the capricious Plymouth turned off on the fringe of Brentwood and headed into an apartment area.

Here was the six-unit apartment house Gus had owned; in one of those units he had died. And right in front of the building the gray Bentley sedan was parked.

Did Barney have another poker game going or was it romance? I parked the Plymouth around the corner and walked back.

It was a two-story building, U-shaped, an apartment on each side of the court and one at the rear on both floors. The only apartment that didn't have a name in the mail slot downstairs was Apartment D. I walked up to see which one that was and came back down to see if there were any lights on there.

It was dark. Romance? It had to be; who plays poker in the dark?

And then it occurred to me, as it often does, that I was overlooking the obvious. There were five apartments in the building that *weren't* vacant.

I ran over the names slowly but nothing registered. I ran over them again and one name rang a small bell. *Veller,* now where had I heard that before? Marie Veller. . . .

It came to me, then, Snip lying on the grass that first time I'd gone to see him. I could hear him saying, "Galbini? He's the bastard that ruined Joey Veller. Joey should have been featherweight champ——"

Joey Veller, who had beat the champ in Mexico, and where was he now? It came to me, he was dead, killed in a car crash. He had been driving and he had been drunk.

And what was Marie to him?

I knocked on her door.

She was dark and small (Filipino?) but not shapeless. She looked at my unimpressive (to her) bulk and up to my face. "Yes?"

"Is Barney here?" I asked.

"Barney?"

"Mr. Delamater."

"Oh— Yes. Come in." She held the door wide.

Barney Delamater sat on a turquoise davenport in the small living room, his bald head glistening under the table lamp next to him, a drink in his hand and a cigar in his mouth. There was no other glass in sight; evidently Marie Veller had not been drinking.

Barney sighed but said nothing.

"I found Al Martino," I told him. "He's in the hospital now."

"So I heard," Barney said. "What do you want with me?"

"Some answers."

He shook his head and sipped his drink.

I looked at Marie Veller, standing quietly near the door. "Was Joey Veller a relative of yours?" I asked her.

"My brother," she said quietly. "What is your name? Who are you?"

"My name is Joe Puma, Miss Veller. I'm investigating the death of Gus Galbini." Then, for Barney to overhear. "He was Joey's manager, wasn't he?"

I turned, as I said that, and saw the surprise in Barney's eyes. Was this a line of inquiry he feared?

Marie Veller said, "Yes, he was. I kept house for Joey. He didn't leave much. So Mr. Galbini let me have this apartment." She paused. "Free. No rent."

I turned my back on Barney to face her. "Mr. Galbini has been good to you, hasn't he?"

She nodded.

"Did the police question you about what happened?"

She nodded again.

"And did you tell them about the free rent," I asked, "and about being Joey Veller's sister?"

She shook her head. "They didn't ask." She looked past me, at Barney, and back. "Should I have told them?"

"It might help. I'm sure you want the police to find Mr. Galbini's killer."

"Yes," she said. "I want that very much."

I took a breath. "But Mr. Delamater doesn't. So be very careful about what you tell him."

From behind me, Barney said quickly, "That's a lie, Puma. You know it's a lie."

I turned to face him. I looked at him but didn't comment.

"I'm here for the same reason you are," he said. "I want to know who killed Gus, too."

"That's hard to believe, Barney. It's too much of a change."

"What the hell do I care about what you believe?" he said. "You're not my keeper."

"I could be an ally," I told him quietly. "You could tell me about the midnight meeting and I could tell you what I've learned and maybe we'd each have more of the picture."

"I don't want any friends," he said, "who put Al Martino into the hospital. I want to stay as far from you as I can, Joe." His smile was purely facial. "Nothing personal. I just don't want to be so close your blood could splash on me."

I stared at him until he looked away. I turned to Miss Veller and said, "If you remember something you think the police should know, the man to see is Captain Apoyan at the West Los Angeles Station. It would be in your best interests to talk to no one but a police officer. Thank you and good night."

I nodded in my courtly way and left without looking again at Barney Delamater. I went out to the Plymouth and waited.

In about half an hour, the lights of the Bentley around the corner went on. When the gray car passed the intersection where I was parked, I swung in a U-turn and let him get a two-block lead.

It isn't much of a trip from Brentwood to Westwood. Both of them are simply realtors' designations; they are part of the municipality called Los Angeles. Barney drove the sleek gray sedan to the small, expensive home in the hills above Westwood, the home of the Lopezes.

He was there for about thirty-five minutes, while I listened to the radio in my car and tried to guess at Barney's real motivation for his sudden interest in the murder.

In his office, I'd received the impression that he didn't even want to *think* about Galbini's death. He still appeared to be as frightened of Al Martino as he was when I first mentioned Al's name. That would indicate he wasn't honestly investigating a murder that would implicate Al. And Martino had been at the midnight meeting in Barney's gym.

When he came out again, I followed once more, all the way to Santa Monica, all the way to his home. The garage door went up automatically as the Bentley broke the beam; it was closing again as I drove past.

The Plymouth seemed to steer herself again. This time, she headed home.

I thought of the dead, Galbini, Veller, and Bugsy Martin —one murder, one accident, one legal execution, all of them equally dead, however. We are all dying, some of us slower than others.

The old prescience again. . . . Driving into my block, an uneasiness moved through me and my weariness went away as I looked up toward my apartment.

Nothing suspicious there; my eyes searched the street for a strange car. There was none on the street in front of the apartment.

But on the nearest cross street, close enough to the corner to command a view of my street, a dark Cad De Ville was parked. Two men sat in the front seat. From there, they could watch the front entrance to my apartment building and the garages in the rear.

I drove past and turned at the next corner. I thought of going back to get the license number, but decided it was too risky. I drove wearily on, to the nearest motel with the vacancy sign glowing. I had forgotten to wear my gun.

chapter seven

IN THE WESTERN VISTA MOTEL A TOILET GROWLED IN THE unit north of me and the occupant of the cell to the south was watching TV, a Western, without the benefit of his obviously needed hearing aid. Outside, car doors slammed and from beyond the parking area came the buzz of Wilshire traffic.

On the hard bed I tossed and called myself a fool. My temper and my trade were not compatible; I was constantly alienating the wrong people. When would I get wise? Hoodlums owned the world; why couldn't I join them?

And then a thought came to me, the first thought that should come to any solid citizen but it hadn't occurred to me until now.

I rose and went to the phone and got the West Side Station. Apoyan or Marty Dugan weren't working tonight, but I talked with a sergeant I knew and who knew my status on this case.

I told him, "It looked to me like a couple of hoods were waiting for me to come home, tonight, so I'm at a motel. Maybe the prowl car could roust 'em a little." I told him which corner to check. "A dark Cadillac, black or blue."

"I'm going over that way, myself," he said, "and they'd better have a reason for being there."

I went back to bed feeling more like a citizen.

The morning was overcast, with a tinge of smog. The morning *Times*, courtesy of the management, had a lot of words on the murder, but no new information.

Before going out for breakfast, I phoned the West Side Station.

Apoyan said maliciously, "The boys tell me you came crying for help, last night."

55

"I asked for the protection that all citizens are entitled to. Who were the mugs?"

"I haven't seen the report. I'll get it and phone you back. Are you home or at the office?"

"I'm at the Western Vista Motel," I told him. "I didn't think it was sensible to go home last night."

He chuckled. "Oh, boy! Puma hiding! I'll call you right back."

Wise guy. He had his badge and ten thousand brothers; why should he know fear? A hoodlum would need to be demented to attack a cop in this town. Up to now.

Outside, the car doors slammed and starters whined as the tourists got ready for the road and the philanderers for their offices. An active hot-pillow trade in these Los Angeles motels. A town of emotional, rootless, adulterous citizens.

I went to the window and watched them leave. Across the court, lonely and elegant, a dark blue Cadillac was parked. It was a replica of the car I had seen last night.

The ring of my phone startled me. I picked it up shakily and it was Apoyan. He said, "Their names are Manny and Jack. They're cousins. Their last name is Lefkowics. They told the officer they were counting traffic on that corner last night. They plan to buy that corner, for a restaurant, if the traffic warrants it."

"Who counts traffic for a restaurant? For a filling station, yes. But a restaurant?"

"The Lefkowicses do, apparently."

"Any record?"

"On Manny, assault. But no convictions. On Jack, for contributing to the delinquency of a minor. No conviction."

"They must have a good lawyer."

"The best—your friend and mine, and Al Martino's—Sylvester Thornton." A pause. "Joe, you're wearing a gun, aren't you?"

"Not right now. If I had been, last night, I wouldn't have had to sleep in this bowling alley. Do you think these mugs have a syndicate tie-up?"

"I doubt it. Joe, you wear a gun from now on."

"I promise. How about the license number on that Cad?"

He gave it to me, and I looked out the window at the car parked across the court. I couldn't make out the digits, but I didn't need to. A fat man and his fatter wife were now putting their expensive luggage into the back of the car.

I went home to shave and strap on the .38. From there, I went to the office.

It could have been my sleepless night, but I doubted it. It was probably the remembrance of the Lefkowics cousins in their big car. Whatever the reason, I was jittery and depressed as I climbed the stairs to my second-floor office.

There was no indication of my office door having been jimmied; some evil person either had a key or a talent for lock-picking.

Because there was evidence in that quiet room that a threatening visitor had come and gone, leaving his ugly, furry calling card behind.

A dead rat was lying in the exact center of my desk.

My vision hazed, cleared, my stomach rumbled. I saw the white slip of note paper next to the rat and forced myself to walk over to the desk.

Two words were crudely printed on the note: *Who's next?*

I was staring at it, lost in a fog of near-nausea when Doctor Dale Graves said from the open doorway, "What in hell is *that* thing?"

I took a breath. "A—warning. Some son-of-a-bitch—"

"You're pale," he said. "You'd better sit down, over there, away from that thing." He pointed at the chair in one corner of the room.

I went over to sit there and he said, "Put your head down between your knees. I'll get you something."

I did, and heard him leave the room.

When he came back, he had a pill and a glass of cold water. He was standing between me and the desk and I didn't realize until he moved away that the rat was gone.

I stared at the desk—and he said, "I got rid of it. I thought I'd better not touch the note, though. Fingerprints?"

"Maybe. Thanks, Dale. I just realized I forgot to eat breakfast. That's probably the reason for my nausea."

"And maybe not," he said. "What was that fuss in here yesterday when the cops came?"

"They were just picking up a hoodlum who threatened me. I'll be all right, Dale. I don't want a lecture, now. I'd rather do what I do than look into dirty mouths all day, like you do."

"You're a fool," he said, "a stubborn and arrogant fool."

"I know. I'm feeling better. I think I'll go out and get some breakfast." I smiled up at him. "You didn't notice anyone messing around my door this morning, did you?"

"No," he said. "It could have been put tl ere last night."

I finished the water and thanked him again. For a few seconds after he had left, I sat where I was, wondering at my weakness. I had never thought of myself as invulnerable but not enough had happened to shake me up this much.

Breakfast helped. My weakness went away; some of my self-confidence returned. It had been purely physical, I told myself, nothing more than hunger, simply my big body crying out for fuel. I was in the wrong business, I told myself further, if a threat from a hoodlum could unravel me.

My stomach growled comfortably and the iron seeped back into my legs. My chin came up and I smiled at the waitress behind the counter.

"You're looking better," she said. "Hangover?"

"Withdrawal symptoms," I told her. "I almost withdrew from the world."

"Who can blame you?" she said. "Some world!"

She was pouring my coffee when Sergeant Marty Dugan took the stool next to me. "Dr. Graves called us," he said. "He told me you were here. I've got the note."

"He worries about me," I said.

Dugan ordered a cup of coffee and looked at me. "We do, too, Joe. At least Captain Apoyan and I do."

"Thanks," I said. "The coffee's on me."

"Do you have to play it so heavy?" he asked gently. "Do you have to be the tough guy?"

"Yes," I answered. "You've got the whole Department behind you, Marty. All I have is my size and my luck."

"Luck or lust?"

I made no comment.

A silence, while Marty sipped his coffee. And then, tentatively, "The Captain thinks it might be a bright idea if I kind of trailed along with you on today's adventures."

I shook my head emphatically. "I'll be all right. I'm armed, now."

"Damn you!" he said. "Damn your arrogance. Do you think the citizens give a damn about you? All those trashy people who crowd Las Vegas, all those slobs spending the grocery money at Santa Anita, do you think they care if you live or die?"

"No," I admitted.

Another silence.

"But you do," I added. "And Captain Apoyan does. And maybe there are a few more citizens we haven't met yet." I put a hand on his arm. "Marty, seriously, *thanks*. And tell that purple-footed Captain I take back every nasty thing I ever said to him."

He sighed. "Okay, Joe. Apoyan told me it would probably be a waste of time. But if you get into a corner, don't call downtown. Just call us at West Side and we'll send a platoon."

He finished his coffee, stood up and put a hand on my shoulder. "In case nobody's told you, lately, I'm glad you're around."

Jeepers! Sentiment from Sergeant Marty Dugan! Cripes!

He went out and the waitress said, "Your eyes are watering. You got a cold?"

"I've got a warm," I told her. "The sun's coming out."

Pure allegory; the day was still overcast and the smog heavier as I walked back to the office.

Next door, Dale's busy drill had started a new day. The mail included a check from Mrs. Lopez and my monthly gasoline bill. I was sitting there, trying to find a pattern, when Hans Mueller walked in.

"Mr. Puma?" he asked, and I nodded.

"Do you know me?" he asked, and I nodded again.

"You're investigating the death of Gus Galbini," he said.

"That's right, Mr. Mueller." I rose and indicated my customer's chair. "Sit down."

He sat down and stared at me stoically for a few seconds and then said quietly, "You've been asking people about that meeting in Delamater's gym."

"Correct. You were there, weren't you?"

"I was." His steady gaze didn't waver. "Mr. Galbini wanted a piece of me, a share in my future. That was what the meeting was about."

"And did he intend to pay for that piece—in money—or in services rendered?"

A pause, while the German studied me. "He half-promised us that Lopez would lose."

"Terry was going to throw the fight?"

Mueller shrugged. "We already knew that Terry Lopez was going to lose, whether he meant to, or not. Mr. Galbini really had nothing to offer us."

"Anyone can throw a lucky punch, Mr. Mueller."

He shook his head. "I've been hit by all kinds of punches, Mr. Puma, but never by a lucky one."

"And Galbini didn't get a piece of you?"

"He got nothing."

"But you didn't report this to the Boxing Commission, did you?"

For the first time, the German's gaze wavered. "I didn't. And neither did my manager. I want to, now, though."

"A good idea," I said. "But ask them to keep it out of the papers for a while. Perhaps you'd better take this story to

Captain Apoyan and have him phone somebody on the Commission first."

He nodded agreement. Then, "Who killed Mr. Galbini?"

"Nobody seems to know, yet. Why was Al Martino at the meeting?"

Mueller shook his head and stared at me candidly. "I don't know. I honestly don't know. Mr. Delamater, now, I got the idea he was a partner of Galbini's, but I can't be sure of that, either."

A silence while we thought our separate thoughts. Then he asked, "Anything else you want to know?"

"Only as a fan. Why didn't you put Lopez away earlier?"

"I wanted to hurt him, to punish him. This trade has been good to me in your country, Mr. Puma. I want to destroy anyone who degrades it."

"Mr. Mueller," I said, "you're more of a citizen than the citizens."

"I'm becoming a citizen," he said. "Why did you put Al Martino into the hospital?"

"Because I love this country," I said, "and I want to destroy anyone who degrades it."

He smiled, and looked less like a German. "But you're in trouble now, aren't you?"

"Nothing I won't get out of." I took a breath. "Once again, an unofficial remark. I've heard you called a storm trooper and a Nazi."

"Yes. And worse. My manager gets 40 per cent of my income. We are very close friends. His name is Abraham Golde. Does that answer the question you didn't ask?"

I stood up. "You go see Captain Apoyan at the West Los Angeles Station. I'll phone him and tell him you're coming."

He stood up. "Thank you." He waited.

I held out my hand, and he took it. He said, "I am strong outside of a ring, too. I learned to fight in the streets. If you need me, to help with these—these evil people, I would be proud to help."

I thanked him. I watched him walk out, a citizen. Two men had declared themselves this morning and the first, Sergeant Dugan, had brought Apoyan's blessing. Against my left breast, the .38 was solid and comforting.

I phoned Apoyan and told him Mueller was on the way over.

And then I sat back and thought of patterns but none came. I went to the window and looked out at the traffic, trying to think. Below, a blonde with a blank face but an impressive figure was looking in the window of a lingerie shop.

On the parking lot across the street, Hans Mueller was getting into his car.

From behind me, there was a scrape of a foot. Startled, I turned.

A dark, short, wide, and malevolent man stood just inside the doorway. He had a scar that ran from his right nostril to his right ear, just missing the eye.

With his left hand, he closed the door and locked the night latch. He used his left hand because there was a gun in his right and it was pointing at my belly. It was a big gun, a service .45.

He stared at me and I stared at him. Against my left breast, my .38 was solid but no longer comforting. I didn't have a chance. If I made a move that .45 would make a noise and I would never move again.

He said, "You bastards never learn, do you? All you cheap peepers are cut from the same pattern. Anything for a buck, huh?"

"Not quite anything," I assured him. "Not suicide." My knees were weak and I kept a hand on the window frame to support me. "I don't remember meeting you before. Are you one of the Lefkowics boys?"

He moved a step closer. "You got a gun. Don't be dumb enough to go for it."

I nodded my agreement.

He asked quietly, "You going to quit? You going to quit—and live?"

"Quit what?" I asked.

"Quit sticking your nose into Al Martino's business."

"I'm not after Al," I assured him, "not personally. I'm investigating the death of Gus Galbini for his widow. I have police cooperation in this and police permission. What excuse could I give them and her for quitting?"

"Al didn't kill Gus," he said.

"If that's true, then I'm not investigating Al."

He took two more steps and now he was close to me. He was smiling and the scar puckered on his cheek. It took a lot of warmth out of his smile.

"You're supposed to be a hothead," he said. "You're supposed to be real gutty. You look scared to me."

"Give me the .45 and let's see if you'll look scared," I suggested shakily.

In his right hand, the gun was steady. His left hand swung in an arc, backhanded, and the force of it twisted my head. He was strong for a short man. In my mind, the redness began to grow.

"You're going to take a vacation, aren't you?" he said. "You're going to get out of town for a while."

I said nothing, trying to quiet the fury growing in me. Bile spilled into my mouth.

He backhanded me again. I almost reached for him, but caution was still in command.

"Answer me," he said.

"If you're one of the Lefkowics boys," I said hoarsely, "the police know all about you. You're acting like a damned amateur."

"Answer me," he said again.

"Put the gun away," I said, "and we'll talk like men."

For the third time, the back of his hand stung my face. I moved toward him blindly—and his gun came up to pause about two inches from my chin. His hand was perfectly steady.

"Don't hit me again," I said. "It's true what you heard about my temper." The hole in the .45 looked as big as a cave.

Another staring session, like adolescents, and I think reason was beginning to take possession of me.

But the idiotic bastard had to prove some kind of point and his hand went over to start another backhand slap.

I had planned what to do in that case.

I was going to dive for the protection of my desk at the same time as I went under my jacket for my trusty .38.

I almost got away with it. My lack of success wasn't due to scarface; it was a misjudgment on my part, and bad footing.

My right foot slipped as I dove for the desk and instead of landing behind it, head down, I came into the corner of it, head on.

All the lights went out and not a shot had been fired.

From oblivion to the haze and the smell of expensive perfume. It was in my nostrils, wet and pungent, physically distressing and emotionally disturbing.

A blonde with revitalizing cleavage was bending over me, mopping my face with a wet and dainty handkerchief. She had a paper cup of water next to her in which she was dipping the tiny handkerchief.

"Florence Nightingale," I murmured. "Haven't we met?"

She shook her head. Her face would launch no ships but her figure would drive sailors mad.

"We've met," I said groggily. "I *know* we have."

She shook her head again. "I heard the rumpus from downstairs. Did he hit you?"

"Downstairs? I know you. You were the girl who was looking at underwear. I saw you through the window before that slob came in. Were you with him?"

She smiled gently. "Don't talk; it'll make your head worse. I was at the lingerie shop and I heard the noise and—"

"You're lying," I said. "You know who he is, and I want to know. He's one of the Lefkowics hoodlums, isn't he?"

"I don't know," she said. "Please don't talk. Are you going to be all right?"

I climbed up slowly to my feet, using the desk as a ladder. She stood up and looked at me anxiously.

"You were with him," I said again.

"What difference does it make? He wasn't supposed to hit you. His boss will hear about that, don't you worry. You're going to be all right, aren't you?"

"I'm going to be all right," I said, "but you'd better stay right where you are until I get the police. What's your name?"

Her bland face stiffened and there was a rasp in her voice. "Florence Nightingale," she said. "You've got one hell of a short memory, haven't you?"

She had a point. I sighed.

She smiled. "Maybe we'll meet again, and we'll get to know each other. Maybe we could even be friends, right?"

"What's your name?" I asked.

"You're pale," she said. "You'd better sit down." She blew me a kiss. "I'm glad you're all right, aren't you?"

She waved, and went out. Her perfume stayed behind and her small, wet handkerchief and in my mind the image of that perfect figure, the D cup Florence Nightingale.

chapter eight

I HAD NO QUESTIONS THIS MORNING FOR MARY LOPER, BUT I wanted to see her. Not only because she was a joy to look at but because I wanted to be sure the malevolent Lefkowics cousins hadn't disturbed her.

She was home, due for an appointment in an hour. She said, "Come in and have a cup of coffee. Where were you last night?"

"Hiding from some hoodlums. Why?"

"I—phoned you. I—was lonely." She looked away, and back. "Are you lying? Is that a story? Were you really hiding?"

"Well, let's say I was avoiding trouble." I came into the kitchen and sat at the small table. "I was avoiding a pair of muscle men who might be working for Al Martino. I—had a little trouble with Al."

She frowned and looked at me fearfully. "Why?"

"He used your name in vain and my temper got the best of me. He's out of the hospital now, though."

She poured me a cup of coffee and sat down across from me. "I haven't seen him since he picked me up in front of the station that morning. Do you think he'll be—bothering me?"

"I don't know, Mary. Call me, if he does."

She nibbled at a sweet roll, her eyes distant.

I asked, "Did you ever meet one of the Lefkowics boys?"

She shook her head. "Who are they?"

"Unconvicted criminals. I haven't met them, either, officially, but I have a feeling I'm going to."

Her hand trembled on the table. She looked at me almost belligerently. "Did you come here to frighten me?"

"Of course not, Mary. I only came over to make sure you were all right."

"And perhaps question me about my brother?"

"No."

"He had a juvenile record," she said. "I suppose you know that, by now."

"I didn't document it. I—heard he had."

She lifted her gaze to stare at me. "You think Terry killed Galbini, don't you?"

"No. I have no prime suspect yet."

"But you think he could have."

I shrugged.

"And that's why you're here," she went on grimly. "To question me."

"That's not why I'm here, this morning. But is there something wrong in my asking you questions, if it would help to find a murderer?"

"If you think the murderer is Terry, it's wrong to use—to use the—the approach you did to gain my confidence."

"Approach? What in hell are you talking about? Cripes, you don't mean—"

"You know exactly what I mean, Joe Puma."

"*Approach*," I repeated dazedly. "What in hell kind of old maid talk is that? You can't be serious, Mary Loper."

"I am," she said. "I was talking to one of your old friends this morning, another Mary, another model—Mary Pastore."

Mary Pastore, my paisan darling. Women.

"Well?" she said.

I took a breath.

"*Well?*" she said again.

"Women," I said, "and their locker room gossip. How did it happen you and Mary Pastore discussed me?"

"You haven't answered my question," she said.

"You haven't asked it."

She colored and that fine chin came up. "You and Mary Pastore, you were—very close, weren't you?"

"We still are. At least I thought we were. We're close friends."

"You're more than that. You're in love with her. Admit it."

"Freely," I said. "I'm in love with her and with you, with a woman named Mona Greene, and a few others. Are you in love with me, Mary Lopez Loper, or still in love with Bugsy? Have I ever criticized you for loving Bugsy?"

"Shut up!" she said.

"Did Terry steer you onto Mary Pastore?" I asked her.

"Shut up," she said again. "The least you could have done is deny that you—that you—well, you know what."

"I haven't denied or admitted anything," I told her gently.

"I try to lie as little as possible. What got you off on this kick?"

"You damned dago tomcat," she said.

"Cut it out," I said harshly. "Please quit acting like the village virgin. It's 'way out of character, Mary."

"Is it? Why?"

I said wearily, "I don't know. The more we talk, the more unreasonable you get. I'm not a rapist. I didn't come here to find out about your brother."

"Sure, sure," she said skeptically. "And last night you slept in a motel. *Alone*, of course."

"Alone," I said. "Hiding from two hoodlums who were probably working for Al Martino and were waiting at my apartment. Al Martino is the hoodlum brother of the deceased hoodlum, Bugsy Martin. And did Bugsy ever suggest marriage?"

"Get out," she said.

I stared at her, and then stood up. "You're being absurd." She didn't look at me. "Leave. Go!"

I stood where I was. "I never mentioned the motel. I simply said I was hiding. How did you know I was at a motel?"

"I phoned the West Side Station," she said grimly, "and an officer told me you could be reached at the Western Vista. Will you please go?"

"I'm on the way. First, though, I want to tell you I learned that the alibi Terry gave the police was a lie. He wasn't at home with his wife when Galbini was killed. I haven't told the police that. Does that look like I'm trying to railroad your innocent brother?"

Surprise on her face and I had a feeling she was about to say something less belligerent than I had heard in the last few minutes.

But I didn't give her a chance to say anything. I turned and walked quickly out.

Women. . . . A single bedroom communication and they want to put you on a timetable. Well, in this case, a double communication, a single *night's* experience. Had I twisted her arm? Had I forced myself on her?

Why hadn't she come right out and asked about last night's motel lodging and the reasons for it? Why did she have to build up her peeve first on the rationalization that I only visited her to find out about her brother. Women!

Aren't they wonderful?

She'd phoned last night; she'd phone again.

The old two-door went chugging along, back to the scene

of the crime, as the phrase goes. Last night, with Barney in the room, Marie Veller had not been very communicative.

The sun was breaking through the overcast now; we could easily have a sunny afternoon. I turned off Sunset as I had last night, and again there was a big car parked in front of the Galbini apartment building.

It wasn't a Bentley this time; it was a Cad De Ville.

I parked around the corner and transferred my .38 from its shoulder holster to my right-hand jacket pocket. It sagged the pocket there but would be easier to reach without arousing suspicion.

I hadn't written down the license number Apoyan had given me this morning, but I had remembered the first three letters—U, V and L. It didn't seem likely coincidence could make this anything but the Lefkowics Cadillac.

A brassy taste in my mouth and some tightness in my throat but I went resolutely to the Veller unit and rang her bell.

I had heard voices from behind the door before my ring. A silence now, not even the sound of a footstep. I rang again.

A man's voice said, "You'd better answer it, Miss Veller."

"What if it's the police?" she asked.

"You'd better answer it."

She opened the door and I smiled at her as she looked at me doubtfully.

"Remember me?" I asked her. "Joe Puma. I was here last night. Could I speak with Manny and Jack?"

They were both shorter than I was, but equally broad. One of them was the scarfaced man who had come to my office. His cousin was as dark as scarface, with a badly pockmarked complexion.

"Manny and Jack," I said cheerfully. "The happiness boys. Figure this would make a restaurant corner?"

The scarfaced one said, "You never learn, do you? What do you want now?"

"I wanted to tell you that your brother had been buried, the one you left on my desk. He's probably cremated by now, at the city dump."

Scarface smiled. His cousin said, "We're busy now, Puma. Wait outside. Miss Veller has some things to tell us."

Marie Veller shook her head emphatically. "That is not true. I have nothing to say, nothing to tell anybody."

Scarface continued to smile. "Not even for money, Miss Veller, a lot of money?"

She shook her head again and looked at him evenly. "I don't trust you two."

"A wise decision," I told her, and looked at them. "Goodbye, boys."

They looked at me scornfully.

I took out the .38 and pointed it in their general direction. "Goodbye, boys."

Their scorn evaporated. Scarface said, "You got no authority to order us out of here."

"Miss Veller wants you to leave. That's authority enough."

They looked at her and she nodded. They looked at the gun and then at each other. They went past me and out.

When the door had closed, Marie Veller said, "I don't want to talk to you, either. I have nothing to say."

"I'm working with the police, Miss Veller. You can confirm that by calling Captain Apoyan. Don't you want Gus Galbini's murderer to be found?"

"Why should I?"

"He was good to you, wasn't he? He didn't charge you rent, remember."

"I've been thinking about that," she said firmly. "The money he made off Joey, he could still owe me more than rent."

"You? Joey did the fighting. Mr. Galbini didn't owe *you* anything."

She looked at me stubbornly. "Please go."

"I don't want to," I said. "I wish you'd listen to me. Your life could be in danger, if you don't."

She looked fearfully at the gun, still in my hand. I put it away.

"Please go," she repeated. "I don't want to talk. I'm sick of talk."

"Maybe," I persisted, "Mrs. Galbini would be willing to pay some money to——"

"Go," she said. "Go, go, go!"

I wasn't the most popular man in the world with the ladies today. I took a deep breath, considered some more words and decided not to voice them, but to watch this place from now on, or to watch her, wherever she went. This was the first sign of an important break in the case.

"Okay," I said, and went to the door.

There, I turned, but she hadn't moved and it was clear she wasn't going to say anything. I opened the door and stepped out, and turned once more.

And was suckered as stupidly as a TV P.I. I heard a rustle

to my right, looked that way—and the other cousin sapped me behind the left ear.

I can't believe he had enough touch to plan it that way, but the belt he gave me didn't send me to the floor. I was still erect, on rubber legs, my sense of balance precarious, my logical mind worthless.

They steered me like a robot to the Cad, into the back section. And one of them said, "On the floor, face down. Or you die now."

I believed him. I did as he ordered.

One of them climbed into the rear and used my back for a footrest. The other got behind the wheel.

I thought of reminding them that kidnaping could bring the death penalty, but decided it wasn't the time. I turned my mouth away from the dusty carpeting on the floor and cursed my intrinsic stupidity.

I should have considered the probability of their waiting for me outside. I should have realized these men had a mission and I was the target. I almost deserved what I was likely to get.

My head was clearing a little and I wanted to get up, to make a stand, to inflict some damage. Purely emotional, this suicidal impulse; my rational mind won out, fortunately. I remained prone and quiet.

Neither of them said a word. They had probably done all their planning while they were waiting for sucker Puma to come out of Miss Veller's. The big car purred along through traffic in a direction I couldn't determine.

We turned and the sound of traffic diminished and the man above me said, "In the back, you know, off the alley."

"I know," the man in front said.

We turned again, more abruptly and there was a slight bump, as though we had driven over a low curb, another abrupt turn and the big car came to a stop.

Above me, the cousin got out, stepping on my ankle in the process. He said, "Up and out, Puma."

I got to my knees and saw the driver was on one side of the car, his partner on the other. I scrambled out, my legs still weak.

There was a U of building around this back court and a dead-end alley squaring off the U. Perhaps it wasn't an alley, but a service driveway. I could smell food and I turned toward the smell to see a row of enormous garbage cans next to a door that could only be the service door to a restaurant.

What must have been a gun prodded me in the back and the pock-marked cousin said, "Follow him."

"Him" meant his cousin, who was heading for a latticed fence at the rear of the building, about fifteen feet to the left of the door with the garbage cans.

The fence was L-shaped and effectively screened what was behind it from the casual gaze of any person in the alley. What was behind the fence was a steel door set in a steel frame.

The man in front of me put a key into the middle of this door. The key evidently didn't open it; as he turned it I could hear a buzz inside the building. He took the key out again, and we waited.

Another buzz, and an amber light went on over the door. He reached now toward the knob on the right side of the door and opened it.

There were steps ahead of us. Halfway up, I heard what sounded like a radio. It was giving the results of the sixth race at some track. This early? I thought, and then realized it was probably an eastern track and the time differential could be as much as three hours.

A bookie joint?

We came up, finally, to a hallway and the man ahead turned to the left. I stole a glance to the right and saw a big room at that end of the hall, and a number of telephones on a long table. It could have been a boiler room for phony stock promotion, but I was sure it wasn't. Only one man was in sight, using one of the phones.

We went past two closed doors to the door at the left end of this long hall. The man ahead of me opened it and stepped aside for me to enter.

There was nothing in this room but a cot. There was no window, only an air vent in the ceiling. The door through which I entered was metal-sheathed, like a fire door.

I was still looking at the cot when the door closed and I was alone. Outside, I heard a noise that sounded like a bar being put across the metal-sheathed door.

For a moment I thought they had forgotten to take my gun because I hadn't remembered them frisking me. But the gun was gone; one of them must have taken it when I was still punchy from the sapping.

I went over to sit on the cot, to light a cigarette and consider the potentials of my possible future.

They had kidnaped me. That could get them the death penalty. I knew who they were; if released they knew I would identify them. What future *could* I have?

My hands trembled and my cigarette dropped to the floor.

I picked it up slowly, fighting for calmness. Bigmouth Puma. Big mouth, big nose, big muscles; small, quiet goodbye.

No! Not yet. I was breathing. My balance was almost back, most of my strength. Think, Puma, *think.* . . .

If this was a syndicate operation, there might still be time for a deal. If it was an Al Martino local, I was due for some lumps. He wasn't likely to forget his trip to the hospital.

The walls must have been soundproofed. It was like a tomb, that room, remote and quiet. I rubbed the ankle that had been stepped on and tried to plan my moves.

How could I plan without knowing theirs? It would have to be extemporaneous and it would have to be instinctive and fast. Surprise was the only weapon left to me.

A rasp broke the quiet. The bar was being lifted on the other side of the door. The door opened, and Al Martino came in.

His soft eyes were blank and his voice controlled. "You wouldn't listen, would you?"

I looked past him to where the pock-marked cousin lounged in the doorway. I looked back at Al and said nothing.

"Ready to listen now?" he asked.

"Have I another choice?"

He nodded slowly. "But it would be a pity, at your age."

"To die? What other choice have you? Your boys kidnaped me, Al. That could easily mean the death penalty. The way I see it, you just have to bump me."

He shook his head, his brown eyes studying me. "Not if you're willing to say they didn't kidnap you."

"Even if I promised," I said, "you wouldn't trust me to keep the promise. Why shouldn't I lie to you, sitting where I am?"

His face was stiffer and his eyes less blank. "Christ, you've got a lot of mouth!"

"What do you want me to do, beg for my life?"

"Do you think I couldn't bring you to that, if I tried? I can make you one hell of a lot less man than you are right now, Puma."

I didn't argue. I looked at the floor.

"Maybe you've never been worked over by experts," he said. "I can get all the experts I want, in five minutes."

He had called me mouthy, but listen to him. Why was he talking so much? I looked past him at the quiet man behind him and thought of the steel door downstairs.

"What do you want from me?" I asked.

"I want you to forget all about that Mueller-Lopez fight. I want you to stop asking questions."

"The fight doesn't interest me," I said. "Only the murder."

"That's a lie," he said. "What did that meeting in Barney's gym have to do with murder?"

"I don't know, but I'll bet you do."

He shook his head. "I don't know anything about the murder."

"Why are your boys bothering Miss Veller, then?"

"For the same reason you are, to find out who killed Gus. And if we find that out, maybe the law will stop digging into the rest of my business."

"Your business?" I asked. "You mean, you're the new local boxing king?"

He stared at me and didn't answer. He wanted to be, that was probably it. With the Feds breaking up the national ring, Al Martino had seen a big, fat, lucrative opening in the local picture and he was moving into it.

"I can't promise you anything, Al," I said finally. "The police already know about that meeting in Barney's gym. They got it this morning from one of the men who was there."

His sleepy eyes widened. "Barney?"

I shook my head.

"Not Golde," he said, "and Galbini's dead and I sure as hell didn't tell 'em." His eyes narrowed again. "Not that Kraut?"

I shrugged.

"Talk, Puma," he said.

The man behind him said, "Easy, boss. Who else but that Berlin blockhead? Puma doesn't have to tell us. We know."

Al turned to look at the stocky man. "I'll do the thinking."

The pock-marked face showed nothing. "Sure, boss. But *do* it. You're telling him more than he's telling you."

I chuckled.

Al flushed. He turned to stare at me. "What's funny?"

"A second lieutenant trying to act like a general."

This time, the cousin chuckled.

Al whirled and his voice was harsh. "You know, Manny, I don't really need you."

Manny's smile was calm, "You sure as hell don't. I figured, being Bugsy's brother, you'd know your way around. But Jesus, the way you're messing this deal——"

A silence, while they stared at each other. Al was the boss, in a way, but unarmed. Manny was the underling, but armed. These thoughts must have gone through Al's mind. Al's brother was dead, but Manny's cousin was alive—and also armed.

Finally, Martino said, "All right, brain—how would you handle it?"

He had tried to be a general and wound up a corporal. And Manny knew it.

Manny said calmly, "We could take Puma about halfway to Catalina and tie a cement block around his neck. Or we could get him to promise to forget the kidnaping gimmick."

I said, "I like that last part better, Manny. I could tell the law I asked you guys to bring me to Martino and you did."

"You don't have to tell them anything," Martino snapped.

I said patiently, "Yes, I do. I'm in business. I'm not in public business, like the police, but there is only so much I can lie about, or get out of the business."

"Who cares if you stay in business or not?" Martino asked.

Manny answered for me. "He's entitled. As long as he stays out of ours. Next time he gets into ours—" He smiled and stared at me. "I'll bet you can't even swim."

"Not very well," I admitted. I stood up and stretched.

Al asked, "Where do you think you're going?"

"Halfway to Catalina or back to my car," I answered. "It's not my decision to make."

Manny chuckled again. "I wish you were on our side, Puma."

"I never will be, Manny," I said.

He nodded thoughtfully, looking between Al and me. And then said musingly, "Wops— Who can figure wops? C'mon, I'll take you back to your junker."

chapter nine

DOWN IN THE COURT, JACK GOT BEHIND THE WHEEL OF THE big car and Manny said to me, "You'll have to lay down again. I'll keep my feet off of you, this time."

"Thanks," I said. "This is a fifty-buck suit."

He shook his head. "A fifty-buck suit and a six-year-old junker and a two-bit office. A man with your guts—it sure as hell beats me."

"It's a disease," I explained, "called honesty."

"I know," he said. "We got an uncle like that, huh, Jack?" He put a hand on my back. "Get in, get down, and shut up."

I didn't make the entire trip on the floor, this time. After we were well away from the neighborhood we'd left, Manny said, "Okay, Puma, you can get up now."

I straightened up and moved into the seat beside him. He handed me my gun and then the cartridges which he had removed. I put the gun into my holster, the cartridges into my jacket pocket.

From the front seat, Jack said, "What happened up there?"

"We'll talk about it later," Manny said.

In the rearview mirror, I could see Jack's glance meeting Manny's. I gave my attention to the passing cars. We were on Wilshire, heading west toward Brentwood. The place we had come from was therefore closer toward downtown.

There were a zillion restaurants in western Los Angeles; I would probably never see that steel door again.

"You're quiet," Manny said.

"For a change," Jack added.

"I've been thinking about Al," I told him. "He's not really a pro, is he? Bugsy was."

"Bugsy's dead," Manny answered. "You worry about your problems, Puma, and we'll take care of ours."

74

I went back to watching the traffic, glad to be alive, looking forward hungrily to a big lunch.

The car swung off Wilshire and went whispering down the tree-lined side street toward my car. We were moving briskly; Jack didn't see the Department car ahead of mine until it was almost too late.

Then he hit the brakes and the tires squealed.

"Keep going," Manny ordered. "Park behind Puma's car."

"You crazy?" Jack asked. "You can't trust that peeper, Manny." He turned around. "He's got us cold; we couldn't beat this one."

"Park behind Puma's car and let him out," Manny said.

It was too late, now. Sergeant Marty Dugan had stepped from the curb behind the Cad and he came up to show his belligerent Irish face in the window next to Jack.

He had a gun held high and he motioned for Jack to lower the window. The power window slid down noiselessly. Sergeant Dugan leaned in and grinned at me.

"Cold, huh? Kidnaping, right, Joe? Thornton won't beat this one."

In the great silence that followed, I said, "I wasn't kidnaped."

Marty's eyes narrowed. "Don't lie, Joe. That Veller woman saw it all. You were sapped." He reached in and took the keys from the ignition. "Get out, all of you."

We got out slowly and stood in a row on the curb side of the Cadillac. A uniformed officer was there, now, his gun drawn.

"Turn around," Dugan said harshly. "Put your hands up on the top of the car."

"This is silly, Marty," I said.

"Shut up and turn around!"

The three of us turned and he relieved us of our guns. We turned back, as a detective I knew only slightly came over toward us.

"Get that woman out here," Marty told him. "I want her to identify these men."

Cars were slowing, their occupants rubbernecking. The uniformed man went out to wave them on. On the sidewalk up the street a ways, a knot of citizens had gathered.

"Marty," I said, "get some dignity. We could do all this down at the station."

He glared at me, all friendliness gone. "For the last time, Puma, shut up!"

I inhaled and stared at the sidewalk.

"You couldn't lick 'em," he said, "so you joined 'em."

I looked up and stared at him. I thought of his visit to me this morning and felt shame.

"Or maybe they scared you," he went on. "You were scared enough this morning."

"I was hungry this morning. I'm hungry now. How long will this farce last?"

His face tightened and he took half a step toward me. There was a tense moment all around and then Miss Veller came along the sidewalk, a shawl over her shoulders, her thin face anxious. The detective was with her.

"Are these the men you told us about?" Dugan asked. "Would you identify them?"

For a split second, Miss Veller's glance rested on the gleaming Cadillac, as though in speculation. I don't know what she was thinking but she could have been thinking about the money Jack had mentioned when we were all in her apartment.

Whatever she was thinking, nobody was prepared for what she said. She said, "I think I recognize Mr. Puma. These other men I don't know." Her look at Marty was innocent and anxious. "Isn't the tall one Mr. Puma?"

He said quietly, "Miss Veller, you know them all, all three of them. I want the truth. You don't want trouble and I want the truth."

Her chin went up. "Whose truth? Yours or mine? I'm telling you *my* truth."

"One more chance," he said grimly. "Who are they?"

"I think the tall one is Mr. Puma," she said. "He is a friend of Mr. Delamater's."

The detective said, "Why don't we take all of them, including Miss Veller, down to the station, Sergeant?"

Marty said nothing, nor did he move.

I said, "And then Thornton will come down and Apoyan's blood pressure will go up again, and what will be gained?"

Marty said, "Thornton? Will he be representing you, too?"

"*Never*," I said.

"Why not?"

"I'm not a hoodlum, Marty."

"Prove it," he said.

"Look it up," I said. "Half the stations in town and downtown, too, look it up."

"Anybody can change," he said.

I said nothing.

Manny said, "Whatever we do, let's do it quick. I don't like to be stared at by all these damned yokels."

Dugan ignored him. He said to me, "I suppose you made

some kind of deal. They gave you some information and you promised them secrecy."

I shrugged.

"A promise to scum like this," he said, "doesn't have to be honored."

I said nothing.

Miss Veller said, "Is that all? I'm getting cold."

"You can go," he said.

She went back toward the house and Marty took the Lefkowics guns from his pocket. He threw them on the grass of the parkway in front of their feet. "Beat it. And stay out of my sight."

They picked up their guns and climbed back into the Cad. Nobody said anything as they drove away.

When they were out of sight, Marty handed me my gun. "Empty, huh? All right, let's have it now. They're gone."

"You know better than that. I have to work my way. Unless I want to go out of business or die suddenly, I have to work a special way. But don't ever be confused about what side I'm on. Are you hungry?"

"I haven't had lunch," he said. "Why?"

"I'll buy you a hamburger," I said. "I want to talk about some angles."

He looked at the detective and the man nodded. "I'll carry on here."

As we walked over to my car, I asked, "When did Miss Veller phone you?"

"About ten ten minutes ago. Why?"

Ten minutes. She had waited long enough.

I didn't answer his question. I put a hand on his shoulder. "We'll talk over the hamburger. I'm so hungry I'm sick."

He shrugged off my hand and stepped into the Plymouth.

We went to a drive-in but ate inside, at the counter. I ordered four hamburgers and a double order of French fries; Marty had a cheeseburger.

Without in any way indicating I had been kidnaped, I told him about the restaurant and the rooms above with the phones. And I said, "It looks to me like Al Martino wants to muscle into the local boxing picture. Maybe Barney Delamater will be a partner, or maybe just a stooge."

"Where is this restaurant?" he asked me.

He'd backed me into a corner. Could I tell him I'd made the trip on the floor of the Cadillac?

"Well?" he prodded.

"When I told the boys I wanted to see Martino," I answered, "they said they'd take me to him, but I couldn't watch the route. I kept my eyes closed."

He used a vulgar word.

"I couldn't even tell you what the front looks like," I went on. "We came in at the back entrance, through a steel door behind a lattice work fence. It was a U-shaped court off a dead-end alley, somewhere on the west side of town."

"You went through all this in ten minutes?"

"Miss Veller lied about that," I said, "and she's the one I want to talk about. I want a round-the-clock surveillance on her."

"From *us,* I suppose? While you're out hobnobbing with hoodlums—"

I said nothing, annoyance growing in me.

"Give me one reason," he said bitterly, "why we should cooperate with you."

"Because I can't watch Miss Veller twenty-four hours a day. Even I have to sleep and eat and go to the bathroom."

He munched on his cheeseburger. He sipped some coffee. He said nothing.

"I have a very strong hunch," I explained, "that she's planning blackmail. It's our first break, Marty."

"In your opinion," he said. "You're not running the Department. We already have a choice suspect." He paused. "We learned something about Terry Lopez."

"What?" I asked, though I knew the answer.

"He didn't go home after the fight. His alibi is cracked."

"He admits it?"

Sergeant Dugan made a face. "He won't even admit his name. We got this from—one of our informants."

"You got him in custody?"

"Not yet. We're doing to him what you want us to do to Marie Veller. He's *our* break."

"Why watch him?"

"Because he's probably tied up with your friends, with Martino and his torpedoes. When we get that tie-up, we've got a case." He paused. "On *all* of them."

I didn't argue any more with him. He wasn't in a reasonable mood.

After dropping him off, I drove to the nearest drugstore to call Apoyan, but he wasn't at the station. I thought of going back to begin my vigil on Marie Veller, but it seemed logical to me that she wouldn't be contacting anyone so soon after a visit from the police.

I called my phone-answering service and was told that

Mary Loper had phoned at one o'clock and would expect a return call. It was now three.

I phoned her; there was no answer.

Had she, I hoped, regretted her cruel treatment of me this morning, her unjustified jealousy? Or did she have something important to tell me? With the new police interest in her brother, it was possible she wanted to talk about him.

Perhaps she figured I had a pipeline into Headquarters, that I had some influence that might get her brother off the hook. No, that was unfair and absurd. My attitudes were too cynical from constantly dealing with the wrong people.

I went back, intending to park somewhere near the Galbini apartment house so I could watch Marie Veller. Instead, I saw her when I was still two blocks from her place. She was walking toward San Vicente.

I gave her two blocks and kept her in sight all the way to the grocery store in the small shopping district off the Boulevard. Here, I waited until she went in and watched to see if she was taking a basket.

She was and that meant at least ten minutes of shopping. I went into the liquor store next door, to phone Apoyan again.

He was in, now, and he said, "Sergeant Dugan told me what you wanted. I can give you one man for one night, tonight, from six until six tomorrow morning. And *that's it.*"

"Don't say you're giving him to me, Captain," I told him. "I get paid whether this case is ever solved or not."

"All right, I'm not giving him to you. But that's as far as I can go, just the same. And I shouldn't do that. I haven't half enough men for this kind of operation."

"Okay, Captain. I'll handle it until six, then."

The call had only taken a minute; I phoned Mary again and was lucky, there, too. She was home.

She said, "I want to talk with you, about Terry."

"I'll be busy until six, Mary. Can't you tell me over the phone?"

"Not—exactly," she said. "Six o'clock? If we're friends again, you could come here for dinner."

"We're friends," I said. "See you a little after six."

Mary and I were friends again, but I had lost Sergeant Dugan. It was a fair enough trade. I went out to the car.

In about ten minutes, Marie Veller came out with her groceries and started walking toward home. I followed discreetly.

It was now three-thirty. Not another soul entered or left her building until almost five o'clock. And then a Pontiac convertible pulled up in front of the building and Mrs. Galbini got out of the car and went in.

I sat where I was for five minutes and then walked over to climb into the front seat of the Pontiac.

In another ten minutes, she was out. She opened the door of her car on the street side, saw me for the first time and drew back.

"I didn't mean to startle you," I said. "Were you in to see Miss Veller?"

"I stopped in there," she admitted. "I came to see Mr. Thompson on the second floor. He's two weeks behind; his rent was due on the first." She slid in behind the wheel.

"Why did you stop in to see Marie Veller?" I asked.

"Because she knew Gus better than any other tenant in the building. And she knows more about what went on in that place than any other tenant. I thought she might have seen something the night it happened, something she didn't tell the police."

"She probably did," I said. I told her about my morning.

"Lefkowics," she said, frowning. "I never heard Gus mention that name." She looked at me anxiously. "Is this—do you run into these kind of people in all your—cases?"

"No. But I usually do, when murder's involved. What did Miss Veller tell you, if anything?"

"She told me to leave. She said she was too nervous and sick to talk to anybody. We'll see if her attitude changes when I cut out the free rent."

"Was it completely free?" I asked. "Maybe Miss Veller just didn't pay in cash."

She shrugged. "Who knows, with Gus? Though he had better than *that* at home. Or am I wrong?" She looked at me frankly.

"You're right," I said. "But men are strange creatures."

She sighed. "Don't I know it? Are you—watching Miss Veller?"

"Until six. Then the L.A.P.D. will take over. I think she could be a key to this case."

"And after six?" she asked me, and her gaze was even franker.

"Right after six," I said embarrassedly, "I have an appointment with an—informant. For a hundred dollars a day, Mrs. Galbini, I feel I ought to put in more than eight hours."

"A *female* informant, probably," she said. "Well, for a hundred a day, I suppose I have no right to expect more than investigation. Carry on, big boy." She started the engine and stared straight ahead.

I climbed out and said, "So long."

She nodded, without turning her head, and the Pontiac took off with a squeal of tires.

I went back to my heap reflecting that Mrs. Galbini was now a well-to-do widow and I was a damned fool. And also it came to me that Mrs. Galbini had a very strong motive herself for the murder of Gus. Money, money, money, money, money.

The rest of my watch was uneventful. At a little before six, a Detective Schultz appeared.

I asked, "You boys don't put in twelve hour shifts, do you? I suppose there'll be somebody else here in the morning, when I relieve."

"There may be somebody else," he said. "I work until midnight on this, unless Sergeant Dugan needs me on that Lopez stake-out."

"Captain Apoyan," I protested, "promised me twelve hours coverage here."

"Beef to him, then," he said wearily. "I just follow orders."

I should have beefed, but I didn't. I was looking forward to seeing my Mary again and fed up with beefing.

chapter ten

ON THE RED BRICK PATIO, THE CHARCOAL WAS ALREADY lighted and on the door a note said: *Martinis in the refrigerator. I'm in the shower. Mary.*

I went into the kitchen and found the pitcher of martinis. I poured one over a whole tumbler full of ice cubes and listened to the sound of the shower through the thin walls, the shower caressing that slim and lovely body.

It became too much for me, this auditory voyeurism, so I took my drink out to the patio and relaxed on the chaise longue.

There were no pink clouds tonight, just the cool breeze coming from the ocean and the yellow pallor of smog to the east. From this height, I could see over the top of it, like a yolk-heavy frosting on a cake.

The faces of all of them went through my mind, the beseeching, the bedeviled and the bellicose faces I met in my constant merry-go-round. Such a wearisome way to make a living, listening to their lies and threats and gossip.

Mary wanted to talk about Terry. I wondered if she wanted to tell me the worst kept secret in town, that his alibi was cracked.

I remembered Sergeant Dugan in my office saying, with his hand on my shoulder, "Joe, if you get in trouble, just call us at the West Side Station and we'll send a platoon." I had asked for one man and they had bitched and finally sent a man subject to being called away.

Words, words, words, words, words.

What was it to me, the death of Gus Galbini? Why did I work tonight?

"Quit muttering," a voice said, and I looked up to see Mary smiling at me, a drink in her hand.

"I'm brooding," I told her. "I only do it about once a day. You look fresh and beautiful." I paused. "And friendly."

She made a face. "I want to take you over to meet a girl tonight."

"Why?"

"Because she asked me to bring you over. Steak, again?"

"You're spoiling me," I said. "Tell me about this girl."

"Not now." She went in to get the steaks.

Friends. . . . We had another drink and ate the steaks, the salad and the rolls. We drank our coffee and talked, comfortable friends. But not this morning, when I'd left. A change in the social climate for the better—and I had to be suspicious of it, because of my trade.

Some impulse in me made me say, "Have you forgotten how angry you were this morning?"

"No. Why did you ask that?"

I shrugged.

Her voice was more edged. "Do you think I'm trying to—to use you?"

"Isn't it natural to wonder why you're no longer angry?"

A pause, and she said, "I talked with Mary again today, Mary Pastore. She says you're friends. No more than that, at the moment, she says. She told me you're not the kind who will *ever* settle for one girl."

"I love her," I said. "And you. Is it time to go?"

We went in my car. Over to Sunset and along its curves to Beverly Hills. Behind the high walls and protective hedges on this fabulous boulevard were the mansions of the mighty, the well-screened abodes of the town's real money.

"Pretty soon, now," Mary said. "That driveway on the right, flanked by those junipers."

A wide driveway, an estate. Far ahead, set in a grove of poplars and oaks, a huge field-stone mansion. *Acreage,* in an area where *footage* is out of reach.

"One of your rich friends?" I commented.

"Not mine," she said. "Terry's." A pause. "Linda Carrillo. Have you ever heard of her?"

"Not Linda," I answered. "The Carrillos, of course, but I've forgotten which half of the city they own."

She put a hand on my knee. "Linda's folks are in Europe right now, and she's worried about scandal. She's a good girl, Joe, a serious, lovely girl, not a scatterbrain."

Linda Carrillo. It couldn't be. I said, "Don't tell me she's in love with your brother?"

"Desperately," Mary answered.

Jeepers! Not a scatterbrain? She had to be, a girl with all

those millions behind her in love with an arrogant and ignorant club fighter. There had to be a big, fat flaw in her somewhere.

The parking area would hold about twenty cars, the garage no more than six. We parked near the front door and went up two wide steps, along the pebbled concrete walk to the front door. I had no chance to ring the bell. A maid opened the door. had no chance to ring the bell. A maid opened the door.

"Miss Loper and Mr. Puma to see Miss Carrillo," I said.

The maid nodded, and stood aside. "Miss Carrillo is expecting you."

We went into the entry hall and followed her past what looked like two living rooms, a dining room and a bathroom to an immense house-wide room in the rear, lofty and walled with planters and one mammoth aquarium wall. The entire place was cove-lighted and the rheostat must have been set low. It was dim in here.

A girl rose as we entered and came over to meet us. Her hair was black as jet, her beauty Castilian, classic and serene. She seemed very young but her poise was enviable.

"Mr. Puma?" she asked, and I nodded.

"You've worked for Mona Greene?" she asked me, and I nodded again.

"And Fidelia Sherwood Richards?" she asked.

I nodded, and glanced at Mary.

Mary said too sweetly, "Oh, Joe knows all the girls."

Linda Carrillo's smile was dim. "Mona and Fidelia claim you're—incorruptible, Mr. Puma."

I shook my head. "Nobody is."

Mary said, "This is beginning to sound like one of those corny TV dramas. Mr. Puma's as incorruptible as he's permitted to be." She paused. "Except around women. He's the corrupted man of the year, there."

I ignored that and asked Linda Carrillo, "Why did you want to talk with me?"

"I'm Terry's alibi," she said. "I'm the reason he lied to the police." Some color in her face, now, and a little less assurance in her voice.

"He had to lie?"

She nodded. "We—were at a motel. Because he's married and because of—my parents, he had to lie."

"Because of your parents? How about *your* reputation?"

She said proudly, "I love him. I don't care who knows that. But my parents, I—I mean—"

"Naturally. Miss Carrillo, I don't see what I can do for you. I'm obligated to tell you to take your story to the police."

"To the police means to the newspapers," she said softly. "I can't do that to my parents."

I lighted a cigarette and looked at the aquarium. One fish stared back at me, the rest ignored me.

She went on quietly. "We never for a second thought Terry would be accused of murder. But the police are suspicious of him, now, aren't they?"

I shrugged.

"You know they are," she said. "They're watching him."

"Who told you that?" I asked her.

"Terry. He's seen them outside his house." She gestured toward a chair. "Don't you want to sit down?"

"I doubt if we'll be here long, Miss Carrillo. I can't understand what you think I can do for you."

"You're a *private* detective," she said. "You can talk with the police *privately*. You can learn if they're willing to take a statement from me without leaking it to the newspapers." She chewed her lower lip. "I'd pay you, of course."

Of course. In her mind, anything could be accomplished with money. I said, "The police need the newspapers in this town. They're afraid of them. And the newspapers live on scandal; that's their only solidly selling item. You can't make a deal like that, Miss Carrillo."

"You mean you won't even try?"

I looked at her fine, intense young face and took a deep breath. "I didn't say that. I'm not sure, right now, how I could sound them out, not mentioning your name, without getting them on *my* neck. At this particular time, I'm not on their hit list. I had to lie to them this afternoon and they know I lied."

"You have to try," she said hoarsely. "*You have to try!* He's innocent, and I know it, and if you can't work it this way, I'll tell the police *and* the newspapers."

"Calm down," I said soothingly. "Don't tell anybody anything, yet. I'll phone you tomorrow. You have an unlisted number, I suppose?"

She had and she gave it to me and I put it into my notebook neatly and efficiently. And then she went to the door with us and thanked us both for coming.

A sweet girl. A real prize. And Terry Lopez—Cripes!

Outside, the night was turning cold. Mary said, "Mona Greene and Fidelia Sherwood Richards and Mary Pastore. Do you know *every* woman in town?"

"I hope to," I said, "before I die. Isn't that Linda Carrillo a darling?"

"They're all darlings to you," she said.

"Not tonight," I answered, and took her hand. "Why don't we go to the Crescendo and listen to George Shearing? Do you like him?"

"I don't know him. Is it that quintet they had there last week?"

"That's it. But it's Shearing's piano I go for."

"Didn't you plan to work tonight?"

"To hell with it," I said. "I'm sick of mugs and cops and double-talking citizens. I wish I had been born smart instead of muscular."

"Or rich," she added. "How much do you think a house like this costs?"

"Too much," I said. "Let's go."

The little two-door went chirping down the long driveway. Mary sat close to me, like the high school kids do to each other and I could almost forget I was a stupid and cynical phony in the phoniest town in the world.

Incorruptible Puma. . . . Horse manure!

Shearing helped and so did his boys. The magic piano of the great man went searching for elusive meanings and occasionally wandered onto a rhythmic truth and the boys communicated with him tonight, answering his questions and looking for questions of their own.

The tight knot between my shoulder blades melted and the nagging ache behind my eyes went away and Mary smiled at me, thanking me for bringing her to this peaceful though invigorating place.

And the booze went down and the day went into history.

And later, in her dim bedroom on the low bed, our communication continued, extended to the fleshly spiritual, soared to the sublime and receded to the nostalgically quiescent.

Those are only words; the act can't be described.

Spent, she said, "Professional, aren't you?"

"No. Love makes me ingenious."

"Love— Love means one person, eternally."

"Only in the magazines. I am a big man with big appetites."

"And no roots," she added.

I had roots; this was my native state. By roots, women mean a schedule, kids, and paid vacations and the PTA. By roots, women mean chains.

"Have you an alarm clock?" I asked. "I have to get back to work at six."

She turned on a small lamp and set the clock on the same table for five o'clock.

"I suppose," she said sadly, "that means no seconds."

"Any time," I said. "Call when ready."

She didn't call. But someone did. Now, you can believe it was a dream if you want. I don't. In a restless near-sleep I heard someone call for help and I wakened in the dark room with the chill of death on me.

My peasant's prescience. No, not that; that is foreknowledge, which I believe I have. This chill of death was contemporary and extrasensory; this chill of death was *shared*.

I sat up on the low bed and there was not a sound from outside. A cold perspiration beaded on my forehead, on my wrists. Next to me, Mary breathed lightly and steadily, her long, thin leg lying over mine.

I extricated myself gently and went to the bathroom. I sponged my face with a warm, wet cloth and washed my arms and the back of my neck. The chill was gone but the certainty remained; someone had died, someone I knew.

I thought of that detective, that Schultz who was on the night watch, and wondered if he had been called away.

If this was a shared death, taking a part of me with it, it would have to mean I was partially responsible. The memory of that moment came back and brought the chill along. I went into the bedroom and quietly dressed.

Mary stirred in her sleep and muttered something; I paused in the doorway, but her steady breathing resumed.

Outside, the night was cold and clear. The two-door started complainingly and moved down the street with a great rattle of tappets. I steered her toward Brentwood. It was now close to four o'clock.

The streets were almost completely empty of traffic; I made good time.

There was no Department car in Marie Veller's neighborhood. Detective Schultz was nowhere in sight.

I parked and went into the apartment building. Again, I'm not asking you to believe; I can only relate what I felt. As I approached her door, the hair on my neck bristled and a coldness seeped into my bones, the coldness of the grave.

I rang her bell and waited. There was no sound from within. I tried the door. It was locked. I rang again.

And then I went to an all-night service station and phoned Mrs. Galbini.

"A hunch?" she said sleepily. "Jesus, man, you don't want me to come way over there with a set of keys just on a hunch, do you?"

"Okay," I said. "Just throw them out onto the front porch

and go back to bed. I'll come and get them. I thought this way would be faster."

"A hunch," she said again. "All right, all right—I'm on the way."

She must have really barreled. Because it was about five minutes after I got back to the apartment that she came with the keys.

And as we approached Marie Veller's door, she asked, "What is it? This creepy feeling, what is it?"

"Your peasant awareness," I said. "I've got it, too."

I rang once more and then she handed me the key. I opened the door, and she reached in to turn on the wall switch.

A lamp in the near corner of the room went on, a dim lamp, but bright enough to illuminate the room. Bright enough for us to see the overturned furniture and Marie Veller in the middle of the living room floor.

There was the handle of a knife still protruding from her stomach.

chapter eleven

APOYAN WAS HOME IN BED; LIEUTENANT TRASK WAS IN charge of the station tonight. He was no friend of mine.

In Apoyan's office, he glared at me and said, "Hunch? You'd need a better excuse than that for being in the neighborhood at four in the morning. What kind of fool do you think I am?"

I didn't answer his question. I said, "Captain Apoyan promised me a man there until six. If he had kept his promise, the killer would be sitting here now."

"How do I know he isn't?"

I took a deep breath and fought the rage bubbling in me.

"Why should Apoyan promise you *anything?* Are you running this station now?"

"I'm working with the *sane* personnel here. At your superior's request."

He froze. *"What did you say?"*

"You heard me, Lieutenant. I've had no sleep for a hell of a long time and your bluster is making me sick. Now, either we talk sensibly, or you can make a charge and lock me up."

His voice was strained. "Watch your dirty tongue, I can get your license, Puma, and I'll probably do it."

The door opened and Sergeant Dugan came in, looking like a man walking in his sleep. "We should have listened to you, Joe," he said heavily. "I'm sorry we didn't. God damn it, we should have listened to you!"

"What happened?" I asked.

"I needed Schultz, and—"

Lieutenant Trask said coolly, "Sit down, Sergeant. You look like you could use a rest. I'm trying to get some sense out of Puma."

Marty looked blankly at me and at the Lieutenant and

89

then went over to sit in a chair as far from the Lieutenant as
he could get.

Trask frowned and his voice was even colder. "Start over,
Puma, and start making sense."

"Go to hell," I said. "I want to phone my attorney."

Marty said, "Joe, for Christ's sake, will you—"

Trask raised a hand for silence, his glare on me. "You're
out of business, as of this second."

"Fine," I said. "May I go now?"

"No," he said. He looked at Marty. "Sergeant, what about
yesterday afternoon? Wouldn't you like to ask Puma about
those hoodlums he was riding with?"

Marty shook his head. "No, sir. I understand how he
operates."

Well, we were friends once more, Sergeant Marty Dugan
and I. I smiled at him.

Trask looked between us and then said to me, "Wait outside."

I went out to the corridor and sat on a bench. I hoped
Marty wouldn't get too unreasonable. He wasn't the most
diplomatic man in the world, the only reason he was still a
sergeant.

Trask was a joiner and had come up on politics, not efficiency. Like so many men who don't know their business
he tried to cover his lack with bluster.

No matter how he came up, he was still Marty's superior
and I hoped Marty would remember that.

Damn that stupid Trask! I should be in bed this second.
With Mary Loper.

Sergeant Marty Dugan came out and closed the door behind him. He used a string of foul words.

"Easy," I soothed. "He's not the only slant-head in the
Department. What's the story on me? Has he remembered
only the Attorney General can take away my license?"

"You're back in business," Marty said. "Jesus, what a knot-
head that man is. And a Lieutenant—"

He sat down next to me and lighted a cigarette. "Okay,
Joe, *why were you* over there?"

"Intuition. So help me, that's all. I don't expect you to believe it."

He inhaled a lungful of smoke and looked at the end of
his cigarette. His voice was low. "All right, then—where
were you at two o'clock?"

"With a girl named Mary Loper, in her apartment. We
went to the Crescendo to hear Shearing and then we came

home to her place about midnight—and sat up playing parcheesi."

"Never mind what you were doing. You were with her?" He puffed again. "She'll swear to that?"

"I'm sure she will."

"Loper," he said, and frowned. "Lopez, Loper— That girl friend of Bugsy's?"

"That's right. And the sister of Terry Lopez."

"And, outside of the obvious, what's your interest in her?"

I didn't answer immediately.

"Does she have some information we should have?" he asked.

I paused, and then said, "She took me to someone who has. But it's not information Trask is going to get."

"Why not?"

"Because Trask is a politician and he caters to the newspapers in this town. What I was told tonight is never going to be printed in a newspaper."

"Isn't that a decision for us to make?" he asked me quietly.

"No," I said.

"You're on awful damned thin ice, Joe."

"I always am. That's why I earn more than a Department man. That's what I sell, my precarious position."

"We could bring in that Loper and sweat it out of her."

"Yes. You can always use your muscle when you run out of brains. But you're not going to, are you?"

"You bastard," he said. "You not only get more money; you get more nookie. You lucky slob."

"I'm charming and single," I pointed out. "It has nothing to do with my profession. Is there any coffee around this dump? I'm bone tired, Marty."

"I can imagine," he said. "That parcheesi is a rough game." He stood up. "This way."

We went to a small room, about twice the size of a storage closet, which held three chairs, a table and a fifty-cup percolator.

He poured me a cup of coffee and I added three lumps of sugar. He sat in a chair at the other side of the table and said, "Marie Veller was killed around midnight."

I stared at him. "Then why the two o'clock bit? Were you trying to trick me, Marty?"

He nodded.

I drank my coffee.

"I'm a cop," he said. "I can't afford to be a friend."

"I know. And that's why I have to keep secrets from you

and all your honest brothers. I don't want to give you Terry Lopez' real alibi just yet, Marty."

"How about yours?" he asked me quietly.

"At twelve o'clock, I was just leaving the Crescendo. I'm sure the bartender will remember me, the one named Duffy. Why do I need an alibi? How in hell can you think of me as a murderer?"

"Anybody and everybody," he said. "That—person Mary Loper took you to see, that was a woman, I suppose?"

I nodded.

"That was Lopez' real alibi?"

I nodded again.

"You're not that stupid," he said. "A woman? Probably a woman in love with him? She'd swear he was the King of Siam. Come on, Joe, there's an angle here, somewhere."

He hated Trask. I think he liked me and he hated Trask. But he and Trask shared the badge and that made them brothers. No matter what his personal feelings were, if he had any, I was still the outsider. I was silent.

"All right," he said, after half a minute, "we'll bring in that Loper woman and get it out of her."

"I didn't have to tell you she took me to Terry's alibi. I'm being as honest with you as I can, Marty. And you're taking advantage of it. If you don't think I'm honest, it's dishonest of you to work with me. Stop talking for a few minutes, and do some *thinking*."

He poured another cup of coffee. "I'm too God damned tired to think!"

"And so am I. Why don't we both go home and hit the sack? Around noon, we can get together with Captain Apoyan and talk like intelligent citizens. Neither one of us is up to any more fighting tonight."

"*Tonight?*" he said. "It's six in the morning, Puma."

"And right now," I said maliciously, "I should be relieving Detective Schultz. There's no need to, is there, Marty?"

"Oh, shut up!" he said wearily. "All right, let's both go home. I'll see you here at noon."

We went out together. He went over toward the police parking lot; I went to my car at the curb. He could have been going home, but I still didn't trust him completely.

From a pay phone on Wilshire, I called Mary.

"Damn you," she said. "This alarm I set for you woke me at five and now you call at six-fifteen. What happened?"

"I was called away. There's been another murder."

"Who?"

"Someone you probably don't know. Mary, the police

might want to question you about that girl, the girl you took me to see. Don't tell them her name. Understand? Under any conditions. Demand that your lawyer be present if they insist on questioning you."

"All right," she said. "All right! But why can't you tell me who was killed?"

"A girl named Marie Veller."

"I don't know her. Joe, what's happening? I'm frightened."

"Don't be," I said. "You're safe. I'd come over, but it would look bad if the police came. Now, please don't worry; you're perfectly safe."

A silence and then, "I'll be home at three this afternoon. Will you come over, then, or at least phone?"

"It's a date," I said. "Get some sleep."

"Sleep—" she said. "I'm sorry I ever met you. Sleep—"

I said good night and went back to the car and home. And just before I fell asleep, I thought of that psychic cry I'd heard around four o'clock.

Marie Veller had died at midnight; so much for my cherished peasant intuition. A man couldn't even trust his delusions these days.

It was after eleven before I returned to consciousness. I was still bushed but Sergeant Dugan had said twelve o'clock and my current relations with the Department couldn't stand further strain. I dragged myself from bed and into a cool shower.

A ham omelette, prepared by my own dainty hands, butter-soaked toast and two cups of instant coffee helped the shower bring me back to semivigor. It was only five minutes past noon when I entered Apoyan's office.

He was looking over some reports and he nodded to a chair. I sat down, lighted a cigarette, and looked patient.

"Steak knife," he muttered. "Whose, whose, whose?"

He wasn't talking to me, but to himself. I asked, "What steak knife? Was that a steak knife in Marie Veller?"

"I wouldn't call it that. Did you see it?"

I shook my head. "Only the handle."

"I did. Has a steak knife got a point? Why should it have a point? These boys at the lab—" He sighed.

"Sergeant Dugan here yet?" I asked.

"No. Why? You two planning something cute?"

"He's bucking for captain," I said, "and I'm going to be his campaign manager. Calm down, Captain; you get paid either way."

He glared at me. "So do you. And for what?"

"For services rendered. Have a cigarette."

He shook his head and picked up a pipe. He knocked out the top ash and lighted it and leaned back. "All right, I'm calm now. What about you and Dugan?"

I told him about last night.

His smile was sour. "So Lieutenant Trask thinks you could be a killer. You know, he might be right? What does Sergeant Dugan think?"

"He thinks I should tell him the name of the woman Mary Loper took me to see."

"But you don't want to?"

"Not now. I don't trust Lieutenant Trask with the newspapers."

"Why should anyone connected with this murder get immunity from the newspapers? What right has this woman to special privilege?"

"None, perhaps. But she has a right to expect me not to betray a confidence. And I'll tell you right now there's no threat that can make me betray a confidence until I'm ready to."

He puffed his pipe. "I know that and so does Sergeant Dugan. Unfortunately, Lieutenant Trask assumes all men are created in his personal image. But the Lieutenant is still a member of this Department and we all work together at this station."

"Under *your* orders," I said.

He said nothing.

"Perhaps I'd better work with the downtown boys," I said. "They appreciate me down there."

"Huh!" he said.

Sergeant Dugan came in, nodded at me, and went over to lay some papers on Apoyan's desk. He stood there while the Captain glanced through them.

I asked, "How about Terry Lopez? Is he clear for last night?"

Apoyan nodded and held up one of the papers. "Poker. From ten to three-thirty. At a room in a west side restaurant, a first-floor room, though." He glanced at Marty. "However, remembering your story of the sight-seeing trip you took with your friends, Sergeant Dugan went around to the back of the restaurant. And there was a steel door behind a lattice-work fence."

I stared at him.

Marty said, "In the game, besides Lopez—Delamater, Martino, a couple minor bookies." He paused. "And Doc Golde."

"You tell me what it means," I said.

"It could mean what you suggested—that Martino is moving in to take over boxing. Lopez is probably the man they'll build up. With the right kind of stumblebums, that can be done, you know."

"And you think Galbini was killed so Martino could take over Lopez? No. Martino probably could have bought Lopez' contract from Gus for ten bucks. Gus knew Terry was through; that's why he bet on Mueller."

"We don't know he bet on Mueller. That's just a strong rumor."

Marty said, "A *very* strong rumor, Captain. I believe it."

"Sure. And Puma, here, thinks Mueller is a solid citizen. What was Doc Golde doing at the restaurant, then?"

"Marty or I could ask him," I suggested.

He looked at Dugan and back at me.

"Unless, of course," I said acidly, "you still don't trust me."

Apoyan smiled. Dugan looked at me steadily. Apoyan said, "Don't sulk, Joe. Most private men get even worse treatment. Sergeant, you interrogate Golde."

Sergeant Dugan nodded. "And what about that woman Puma talked with last night, that alibi of Lopez'? Shouldn't Lieutenant Trask be informed about her?"

"I'll decide that, Sergeant," Apoyan said evenly. "I want to discuss it right now with Joe."

Dugan left and Apoyan looked at me.

"Lopez doesn't need an alibi, now," I said. "He's covered for last night."

"You're assuming it's the same killer?"

I nodded.

"That's too much of an assumption," he said. "There's absolutely nothing to substantiate it. I guarantee you her name will be kept from the papers."

"How can you guarantee it, Captain? If you send a man out, he might leak it to the reporters. Or he might try to curry favor with Trask by telling it to him."

"I'm not sending anybody," Apoyan said. "I'm going myself."

I took a breath.

Apoyan said quietly, "You have my promise her name will never see print unless she's criminally involved in one of these murders."

I hesitated, and then said, "Her name is Linda Carrillo."

He looked shocked. "The Beverly Hills Carrillos?"

"Right."

"My God!" he said. "You mean she and that Lopez are——"

I nodded again. "And how can you go into Beverly Hills without consulting with the Department there?"

"I'm not making an arrest," he explained. "I'm simply going in to talk with the girl. Okay, Joe, thanks. Your confidence will be strictly kept."

"Explain that you talked with me," I asked him, "and that she has nothing to fear from the papers. Her folks are in Europe and she's very concerned with the family reputation. She's a good girl, Captain."

"Don't worry," he said. "Trust me, Joe."

I had an uneasy feeling as I left him that I had made a mistake in revealing the girl's name. Like any public servant in this area, Captain Apoyan was subject to an unreasonable and unhealthy newspaper power. But I had to trust *somebody*.

Sergeant Dugan was on his way to see Golde. I went to the same hotel and asked for Hans Mueller.

He had moved from the hotel to an address on the west side of town, I was told, because his wife had come out from the East and they wanted housekeeping facilities. Doc Golde was still at the hotel.

I went out to Sepulveda Boulevard, to a one-bedroom unit in a mammoth apartment development at the National intersection.

A woman answered to my ring, a short, blonde and genial-looking lady of about thirty summers who identified herself as Mrs. Mueller and told me that Hans had gone out to buy a paper and wouldn't I please come in?

I came in and sat on a worn sofa in what was obviously a furnished apartment.

She said, "We've decided to move out here. Our furniture is back East. Is it always warm here?"

"It's warm enough. It's not like Miami," I told her.

She made a face. "Miami—ugh—"

I made no comment.

"Hans has talked about you," she said. "He admires you."

"Thank you," I said. "He's still being managed by Abraham Golde, I suppose?"

She nodded, her light blue eyes searching my face. "Has something happened to Abe?"

I didn't get a chance to answer. The door opened, and Hans came in, a *Times* folded under his arm.

He smiled as I rose and came over to shake my hand. "Mr. Puma, it is good to see you. Have you come for help?"

"Not—*physical* help," I answered. "Not yet. I wanted to ask you about Doc Golde."

He glanced at his wife and turned back to me. "Yes?"

"He was in a poker game, last night," I said.

"I know."

"With some pretty unsavory characters," I added.

He frowned. "Unsavory? I do not know the word."

"Some hoodlums. Al Martino and some gamblers." I paused. "And Terry Lopez. Did you know that, too, Hans?"

He sat down next to me on the sofa. "Yes, I knew that. I think Abe is—afraid of these kind of men. He would never sell me, though, or sell me out. But he hasn't the courage to refuse to talk with them. Is that a sensible explanation?"

I shrugged.

"And he loves to play cards," Mueller went on, "and poker at the stakes they play for is very exciting for Abe."

Mrs. Mueller said lightly, "Birds of a feather—"

Hans Mueller looked pained. "My wife, for some reason, does not share my great affection for Abraham Golde."

"Perhaps," she said, "because I have too great an affection for Hans Mueller. And where is he, today, under the brilliant Abraham Doc Golde's fine management?"

I said, "Your husband, Mrs. Mueller, has a solid and growing reputation. That's what is important; the money will come."

Mueller smiled. "Thank you. My wife has adopted the vices of this country more quickly than the many virtues. She has developed a warm love for money."

Her face stiffened. "That is not true. It isn't the money. It is the championship, the middleweight championship of the world, and I want it not for me, but for you."

He didn't look at her. He asked me, "Is there anything else?"

"Did Doc tell you anything about last night?"

Hans Mueller frowned. "There was nothing—definite planned. Martino suggested another bout for me with Lopez. Abe got the idea Martino is now Lopez' manager. One of the other men, the gambler, said there was still plenty of Lopez money around. Those Mexican fans of his think with their hearts, not their heads." He paused. "That was said when Lopez was out of the room, Abe told me. Abe didn't commit us to any promises, but he didn't say 'no' to anything, either."

A snort of derision from Mrs. Mueller, but no further comment.

Mueller said, "Would you like a bottle of beer, Mr. Puma? I usually have one about this time."

I had a bottle of beer with him. Once the subject of discussion was no longer Abraham Golde, Mrs. Mueller became genial again. It appeared that these two got along well, except for that one thorn.

Hans Mueller impressed me as an honest man, though I had guessed wrong about a number of people on that. At any rate, he served first-class beer.

I thanked him and promised I would call if I needed him. I was going down his walk to the main walk when another principal in this drama came into view.

It was Barney Delamater.

As he came abreast, I stopped walking. I asked him, "Win much last night, Barney?"

"Win much? Where?"

"Playing poker with your hoodlum friends at that restaurant."

He stared at me doubtfully and said nothing.

"With Al Martino," I added, "and Doc Golde. Is Al your new partner?"

"Why don't you give up?" he asked me. "Why don't you take on somebody you can beat?" He pushed past me.

I went down to my car reflecting that he was probably giving me good advice, though I doubted that it was well meant.

chapter twelve

I WENT TO THE OFFICE TO BRING MY REPORTS UP TO DATE and check the mail. Dr. Graves's drill was mercifully quiet and even the traffic from below seemed muffled.

As I typed, I tried to make some sense out of the obvious lies, the denials, the animosities. The only pattern that showed was centered around Martino and the organization he was trying to develop.

But why would Martino need to kill Gus? There was no motive I could see. Certainly not to get control of Terry Lopez; he must have been for sale cheap. And Gus had bet on Mueller *through* Martino and won; what conflict could result from that?

Unless Gus couldn't collect?

What if Gus had really shot the wad on Mueller and Martino didn't want to bring in the loot? Gus waiting there in that apartment of his for the payoff—and getting it in lead.

Had Marie Veller seen Martino go up to the apartment? Had she then heard the shot? Why else would Martino's musclemen be trying to buy her?

And then another thought struck me. I could be wrong on Lopez. He didn't look like a contender to me but I was no fight expert. Lopez, in first-class fighting shape, was something I had never seen in action. Out of shape, even a champ can look like a bum.

Maybe he was a valuable piece of property and maybe Gus knew it. And Martino, not being able to buy Lopez, had. . . . No. If Gus died, wouldn't the contract be a part of his estate? I didn't know. Mrs. Galbini should.

I phoned her and she told me, "There was no written contract. There isn't even a claim I can make. I guess those two trusted each other." A pause. "What have the police learned about Marie Veller?"

"Nothing they've told me."

"There must have been a fight," she said. "I mean—the way that furniture was overturned, and all."

I agreed that was possible.

And then she asked, "Are you getting anywhere? I mean —are you learning anything?"

"Very little, Mrs. Galbini. My conscience is beginning to bother me; I have a feeling I'm wasting your money."

"Well," she said, "*my* conscience would bother me if you quit. Because, you see, it's really Gus's money. Keep plugging."

I hung up wondering about her, trying to fit her into the pattern in the killer's role. Again, no motive. That is, if I accepted her stated acceptance of her place in Gus Galbini's life, jealousy would be out as a motive.

Was I overlooking money? It was a community property state so with Gus alive, half was hers. But Gus, alive, could spend it, too. With Gus dead, it was all hers, and she could save it or spend it according to her whim.

I heard footsteps in the hall and soon Captain Apoyan was framed in my office doorway. He said, "I was in the neighborhood, so I thought I'd drop in."

"In the neighborhood seeing Linda Carrillo?"

He nodded and came over to sit in my customer's chair.

"What did you think of her?" I asked him.

He rubbed the back of his neck. "What should I think? Rich people always look honest and sound honest. We can't imagine why anyone should lie unless they need the money."

"You're being cynical, Captain. You believe her, don't you?"

"Almost. I checked the motel before I *almost* believed her, though. Terry Lopez still isn't completely off the hook, not to my way of thinking."

I said nothing.

"And neither is your client, Mrs. Galbini," he said.

"Why would she hire me, if she was guilty, Captain?"

"To find out if we were getting on her trail. She asked me to recommend a man, didn't she? That could mean she wanted a man who had access to our records and our lines of investigation."

Again, I said nothing.

"What are you so quiet about?" he asked.

"Captain, I've been sitting here, realizing how inefficient I am. It's comforting to learn that the Department, with all those men, is just as frustrated."

He used a vulgar word and stared at the floor.

"Where next?" I asked him quietly. "We're nowhere, aren't we?"

He rubbed his neck and didn't answer. He would never admit defeat, not Captain Apoyan.

"That restaurant where the poker was played," I said, "do you know the address offhand?"

He told it to me, and asked, "What can you do there?"

"Have a cup of coffee and dawdle. See if somebody gets nervous and makes a move."

He shook his head. "I don't understand you. Among people like that your life is not important. You haven't any badge to protect you and you've got the kind of insolence that makes enemies. You sure love to live dangerously, don't you?"

"That must be it," I answered. "I think you've hit it, Captain."

"Hit what?"

"The reason why I stay in this ridiculous business; the danger adds spice to a dull life."

"It's the women that adds the spice for you, not the danger," he corrected me. "Are you really going out there?"

I nodded.

"If you get in a jam, use my name," he said. "If anyone wants to question your authority, you have them call me."

"Friends again," I said. "How sweet!"

He looked at me sourly and stood up. "And try not to get lippy, for a change. Your mouth is your worst enemy."

I nodded and smiled and he went out. It was now three o'clock and I remembered my promise to Mary. I phoned her and let it ring ten times, but there was no answer.

Back to my busy two-door; back to the road.

It was a big restaurant, a low building with a shake roof and enormous parking lot on the Coast Highway, near Malibu. Strange that I hadn't heard the sound of the waves when I'd been brought here. *If* I'd been brought here.

I didn't drive onto the lot; I drove along the asphalt road that serviced the shopping center adjoining the restaurant and found another road leading behind the restaurant. I parked.

This was my dead-end street. This was the place, I felt sure. I got out of the car and walked up the alley. The garbage cans were there and so was the lattice-hidden steel door.

I left the car where it was, on the shopping center parking lot, and walked around the restaurant to the front door.

There was a stack of racing forms on the tobacco counter next to the cashier's register; I bought one and went to a corner booth where I had a view of every table and the entrance.

It is difficult to read a racing form thoughtfully, but I tried.

The waitress came; I ordered coffee without looking up. She muttered something that sounded like "horses, horses, horses" and went to get my coffee.

She brought it; I took out a pencil and paper and began handicapping. Simply protective coverage. In my sly way, I was casing the joint.

There was no face in sight I recognized. About half of them looked like tourists, most of them drinking, not eating. Through the front windows, I could see a few whitecaps and some charter boats coming in from their day's fishing.

Quiet and peaceful in the place as I made meaningless figures on clean paper and drank the excellent coffee.

The first face I knew was a rather distinguished one. A tall man in a highly garish sport coat (for *him*) came in with a blonde—the good Samaritan who had ministered to me in my office.

It was a revealing combination because the tall man was the attorney I had tangled with at the hospital, the eminent Sylvester Thornton. He paused for a moment to exchange pleasantries with the cashier, which would indicate he was no stranger here.

The blonde was obviously bored with this dialogue; her glance moved around the room, settled on me, moved on, and came back.

I waved at her.

She paused for a second and then doubtfully returned my wave.

Sylvester caught her wave, glanced my way, stared at me for two full seconds and then said something to her.

She shrugged.

They walked over toward a booth; I gave my attention to the racing form.

In less than a minute, a shadow fell across my digits and I looked up into the grave face of the barrister.

"You know Miss Chapman, do you?" he asked me.

"Never met her," I answered. "Not that I remember."

He flexed a jaw muscle. "Your first visit here?"

"Only to this part of it. I spent some time upstairs yester-day."

He looked at the racing form and back at the booth, where the blonde was ordering. Then, frowning, "Could I sit down for a minute?"

"Be my guest."

He sat down and took a few seconds to compose his thoughts. Then, "According to your own statement, and other information I have, you are currently engaged in in-vestigating the death of a Mr. Gus Galbini."

I nodded.

"Al Martino had nothing to do with that, believe me," he said earnestly.

"Then he has nothing to fear from me," I said. "So why are you concerned?"

"Because," he answered, "your investigation constantly turns his way. Last night is a case in point. Mr. Delamater told me a little while ago that you knew he played poker here last night."

"That doesn't mean I was investigating Martino. It could mean I was investigating Barney."

"I don't think that's the way it is. Mr. Puma, you have an unusually successful record for a private investigator. You enjoy exceptional police cooperation. Frankly, Mr. Martino wants no trouble with you. But if you pursue the unreason-able course you have followed lately, you are going to run into—resistance. And there is no need to. Albert Martino had nothing to do with the death of Galbini."

"Counselor," I said reasonably, "look at it my way for a second. The woman who could have been the key witness in the murder of Galbini was threatened by a pair of Martino stooges. That same night, the woman, Marie Veller, is killed. Some time ago, another witness was killed by Al's brother and the brother was executed for it. How can you sit there and expect me to take *your* word on the innocence of Bugsy Martino's hoodlum brother?"

"Hoodlum?" he said. "And shyster— You use strong lan-guage, Mr. Puma. What has Mr. Martino ever been convict-ed of?"

"Thanks to you—nothing."

He was silent. I looked past him and saw the blonde dig-ging into a double martini. Her eyes met mine over the rim of the glass. I winked.

Sylvester Thornton said heavily, "You are being extremely stupid, even for a man of your limited mental capability.

You are wasting your client's money and plunging foolishly toward disaster."

I shook my head. "All I'm doing at the moment, barrister, is figuring a horse for tomorrow. The rest is your imagination. Or maybe it's your conscience kicking back to life."

He stood up. "You are doing yourself and your client a serious disservice by not taking my advice."

"Possibly. Give my regards to Miss Chapman."

"Her name is not Chapman," he said. He nodded and went back to her.

Tricky Sylvester Thornton, using a false name, trying to make a tricked witness out of me. I was glad I hadn't told him I knew her when he'd asked.

The waitress came back to ask, "More coffee?"

I shook my head. "I think I'll have a drink of something stronger. How about a Scotch mist?"

She nodded, paused, and said, "You know that's *yesterday's* racing form, don't you?"

"Sure. I'm not really a horse player."

"I figured you might not be," she admitted. "You look too well fed. Scotch mist coming up."

When she came back, I asked her, "Do you know the blonde with Mr. Thornton?"

"I don't even know Mr. Thornton," she answered. "Who's he?"

"The one with the loud sport coat sitting across from the blonde in the white dress."

She turned and looked at them and back at me. "He comes in quite a lot, but I didn't know his name. That blonde gets a hundred a night, more if you're drunk. Is that what you wanted to know?"

"Not at all," I said. "I'm a decent young man. I simply wanted to know her name."

"Everybody calls her Mike," she said. "I don't know any other name for her. She in trouble? You a cop?"

"She's not in trouble, so far as I know. I'm a world-famous movie producer and I'm looking for new faces, that's all."

"You're a cop," she said, and went away.

It was restful, sitting here; I didn't want to leave. I thought back to yesterday's blind trip and realized how wrong I had been in assuming they had brought me back to Brentwood by traveling west. Those Lefkowics cousins were *pros*. And so was that Sylvester Thornton.

How long would they stay under the dominance of a bumbler like Al Martino? Was there a crack in that relationship I could widen?

I finished the Scotch mist and ordered another.

The blonde was nibbling her second double martini and listening with what looked like boredom to the monologue of Sylvester Thornton.

Another familiar face came through the entrance doorway. It was the pock-marked cousin, Manny. He talked for a few seconds with the cashier and headed for Thornton's booth.

He stood next to the table a few seconds there, talking with Thornton, and then must have been told about me. Because he glanced quickly my way, looked back at Thornton and nodded.

I sipped my drink and put away the paper I'd been scribbling on. I was lighting a cigarette when he came to my table.

"You," he said, and sat down across from me. "What now?"

"It's a public place, isn't it? I stopped in for a drink."

He shook his head. "You're crowding me, Puma. Thanks for keeping your promise, but you're getting pushy again."

"Nerves?" I asked him. "What harm can I do, sitting here, drinking?"

He expelled his breath and stared at me. The waitress came over; he ordered a bottle of eastern beer and continued to stare at me.

Then, "One question—did the police learn about the game here last night from you?"

I hesitated, and shook my head.

"I figured they didn't," he admitted. "They followed Lopez, right? That's how they learned about the game?"

"You said 'one question,'" I reminded him. "That makes three."

"Okay." He looked at my glass. "What the hell's that?"

"Scotch and crushed ice. I've got high-class tastes."

He chuckled. "Puma, I should really knock you off, but it would bother me. What makes you so ornery?"

"I'm not. I'm stubborn and single-minded, but I get along with most people, most *decent* people."

"You sure get along with the cops," he said. "That's unusual in your racket."

"One question," I said. "Does Martino really think he can build a nothing like Lopez into a contender?"

His face stiffened. "Who told you that?"

"I answered your one question. It's your turn."

"All right, all right. Yeh, he does. And he can."

"Is that why he had Gus killed, so he could get Lopez away from him?"

"He didn't have Gus killed. He don't know who did. He could have bought Lopez' contract from Galbini for five hundred bucks. He wouldn't have a man killed for a lousy five hundred."

"Okay. Where's Jack this afternoon?"

Manny sighed. "Fishing. He's crazy for that deep-sea fishing. I don't see it, do you?"

I shook my head. "Who's the blonde with Thornton?"

His shrug was too casual. I thought his voice was too casual, also. "Some broad. He's got a different one every night. He's a quiff-hound."

"He gave me quite a lecture," I said, "about the innocence of Al Martino and my wasting my client's money and my time. He's stuffy, isn't he?"

"All lawyers are," Manny said. "He's sharp, though, like a needle. Puma, you're pushing your way into a blind alley. What's boxing to you?"

"Less than nothing," I said. "This time, though, it's tied up with murder. Maybe you don't know it, Manny, but some of your friends know it and that's why I keep getting involved with you. I don't look forward to our meetings."

He chuckled again.

He finished his beer and signaled the waitress. He ordered for both of us. When the waitress was out of hearing, he said, "Al didn't kill Gus. I didn't. Jack didn't. Why don't you start looking somewhere else?"

"Maybe Lopez did," I said, "or Barney Delamater. Or Doc Golde or even old double-talk Thornton. Or maybe you're lying about the others. Or even yourself. I have no other leads, Manny."

"I'll give you one," he said. "The widow. Mrs. Galbini."

I said nothing.

"You in there?" he asked me. "You getting some of that?"

I shook my head.

"She's paying you though, isn't she?"

I didn't answer.

"Because she hates Al," he said. "Because Gus and Lopez didn't have a contract she could peddle. She's paying you to railroad somebody, Puma."

I shook my head.

"Figure it out," he said. "Who comes out of it with the loot? Mrs. Gus Galbini. Who else makes a dime out of it?"

The Scotch was getting to me. I have a low threshold for hard liquor. Manny's features blurred and his voice seemed to be coming through a tunnel from far off.

At some time in the haze, I must have agreed with Manny,

because he became more jovial and insisted on buying another drink. What number it was, I will never know.

And then in my blurred vision, the tall figure of Sylvester Thornton loomed. He looked down on us like Zeus, god of moral law and order.

And clearly I heard this god say, "Al want to see us, upstairs."

"Sure," Manny said. "You wait here, Joe. I'll be back."

They went away.

Now whether the blonde had come to our booth with Thornton or whether she came after he left, I don't know. I do know I smelled her before I saw her. It was expensive perfume but there was just too damned much of it.

And suddenly she was sitting in the seat still warm from Manny and her cleavage came to my attention and I looked up from there into her blank face.

"All by our lonesies, they left us, didn't they?" she said coyly. "That's all right with me, handsome."

"Me, too," I said. "Have a drink."

"I don't want a drink," she said. "I want to get out of here. I don't know what's in that Sylvester's mind, but I don't like it. He wants me to say some nasty things about somebody, and I don't like it. Could we get out of here?"

"Hell, yes," I told her. "My car is on the supermarket parking lot next door. You go there and I'll meet you."

"They'll be mad," she warned me. "Sylvester said I could get into a lot of trouble if I didn't cooperate."

I gave her my keys. "To hell with Sylvester. My license number's on that key ring. We'll go one at a time."

She slid out and moved toward the doorway and I watched her twinkling rump in the white dress shift right, left, right, left, right, left. . . .

I rose with what dignity I could dredge up and carefully followed the path she had set. I doubted that anyone watched my rump.

chapter thirteen

A LOT OF TIME MUST HAVE PASSED WHILE I HAD BEEN gabbing with Manny. Because it was dark out now and the traffic on the far side of the road was heavy, the late sunworshipers coming back from the beaches.

I walked between the parked cars of the restaurant lot to the larger lot near the supermarket and there was the blonde, behind the wheel of my humble car. At a hundred a night, she probably didn't ride in many cars as old as mine.

"I thought I'd better drive," she said. "You're a little drunko."

"I'm more hungry-o," I said. "Is there another restaurant around here?"

"Not a good one," she told me, "but I know a place where we can eat."

A puzzling answer, but I didn't pursue it. The car was warmer than the night air and my haziness was returning. I relaxed in the seat while she steered my battle-wagon down the service road that led to the highway.

If I had eaten, I wouldn't have been this drunk, I knew. I need food like most people need air.

The blonde turned the car north and said cheerfully, "Sylvester will be furious. I don't care, though. I don't like him. Do you like him?"

"No. Who is the person he wanted you to say the nasty things about?"

"Ugh!" she said. "Let's not talk about it. I'm hungry. Do you like fillet?"

"Love it," I said, and the haziness came back stronger.

Deep in me, suspicion stirred briefly. What if Manny and Thornton had planned this, leaving me alone with the blonde,

108

so she could lure me to my destruction? They knew my lures, food and women.

"Why so quiet?" she asked me. "What are you thinking about?"

"Food," I said.

"Soon, soon." A pause. "You're not—going to get sick, are you? This is a new dress."

"Not actively sick," I assured her. "From hunger, only."

The house was on the beach side of the road, on piles that kept it above high tide, a trim little cottage of marine-varnished redwood, set into a sheltering cove.

"Cozy," I said. "Yours?"

"No. Do I look rich? A friend of mine. He's in La Jolla for a couple of days, but I know where the key is."

"Won't he care?"

"Of course not. Any time, he told me. Any time. That's why he showed me where the key is."

I followed her down a narrow wooden ramp that led from the parking area, at highway level, and around the side of the building to a row of flower boxes set below the windows. The sea air was clearing my brain. And increasing my hunger.

"One, two, three," she counted and reached under the third flower box for the key while I waited at the door.

The house smelled faintly damp, from the sea, and there was a scarcely perceptible iodine odor. Like the Lopez home, it was short on size but long on quality.

The front of the house faced the ocean and the living room ran along the entire front of the house, the wall toward the ocean all glass.

In the cove-lighted living room, the blonde called Mike said, "Sit right there. I'll bring you a glass of milk to hold you."

I sat down and she went quickly to the kitchen and just as quickly returned with a big tumbler of milk.

"I had a boy friend like you once," she said. "He got sick when he was hungry. Do you?"

"Yes. You're a saint, Mike. Is that your real name— Mike?"

"It's real enough for you," she said. "Over there, from that chair, you can see the lights of Santa Monica. Why don't you sit over there?"

She went back to the kitchen and I took my glass of milk over where I could watch the lights. I still retained the faintly uneasy suspicion of a possible trap. I was armed, however, so it wasn't a major concern.

From the doorway, Mike called, "I suppose you like it rare."

"Bloody," I said. I finished the milk and went out to the kitchen.

There was a double-door refrigerator-freezer out here, at least an eighteen-footer.

Mike opened the refrigerator door and pointed to about half a dozen steaks in the meat tender. "This week's," she said. She opened the freezer door. The meat was wrapped here; the section was jammed full. "All steak," she said.

"Is that all your friend eats?" I asked.

"Just about. You know what he told me? He said he was a magazine writer for twelve years, and starved. Now, he's selling that TV like crazy and he swears he'll eat nothing but steak."

"One of your—your clients?" I asked.

Her cheeks flushed and her eyes shamed me. "You didn't have to say that. Why?"

"I don't know," I said gently. "I apologize, Mike."

She sniffed. "So he was a client, once. But now he's a friend. He's just about my best friend. I don't think I like you, Joe Puma."

"You shouldn't. I apologize again."

She smiled. "Kiss me, then. Kiss and make up."

I leaned forward. The face wasn't much, but that vintage body pressed close and I suddenly felt a great need for a hundred dollars.

She pulled away—and laughed at me. "Surprised you, didn't I? Get out of my way, now; I'm hungry." She bent over to put the steaks in the broiler.

I went over to sit in a breakfast nook upholstered in what looked like genuine leather.

"Your friend is doing all right," I commented.

She nodded, adjusting the broiler level. "You know what?" He wants to marry me. Isn't that something?"

"You could do worse," I said.

She faced me frankly. "I wouldn't do that to him. And besides, who wants *one* man? I like men. I mean *men,* not *drizzles* like that Sylvester. Gosh, I'll bet he's steaming now, huh?"

"He and Manny and Al Martino are probably all steaming about now," I agreed. "Doesn't that frighten you?"

Her eyes widened. "Should it? What's going on? Is something going on I should know?"

I shrugged. "I'm not in their confidence. Tell me, what did they want with you?"

"I don't want to talk about it," she said. "It was nasty, that's what it was, and I wasn't going to do it, anyway."

"Do what?"

She ignored the question. She picked up my empty glass, filled it with milk and brought it to the table. She sat down across from me and slid the glass across. "Drink. You still look weak."

"Do what?" I asked again.

"You're a private detective," she said. "I almost forgot that, for a minute. Drink."

I sighed. I drank.

"Relax," she said. "Look how cozy we are. Don't be *working* all the time."

"Two people have died," I said. "They were killed. Maybe you could help me find out why they died and who killed them."

She shook her head. "That must be another case you're working on. You must still be drunk." She took out a cigarette. "Light?"

I found a match and lighted it. She leaned forward, across the table, and those perfect breasts were almost completely in view.

"Steady," she said. "How can I get a light with your hand shaking all over the place?"

I had a feeling I was going to get nowhere. In an investigative way, I mean. She had undoubtedly learned, early in her career, not to confide too much in people on my side of the law.

We ate steak and toast and milk and I felt better. She suggested we take our coffee into the living room.

In this dim room, looking out at the lights, it seemed her perfume was no longer overwhelming and the silhouette of her perfect body dulled the memory of her immobile face.

I asked, "How long have you known Sylvester?"

"About a month. I met him through Al. Is Al a—a criminal?"

"Not officially, I guess. Do you like Al?"

A few seconds of silence before she said, "I don't know. He thinks a lot of himself, doesn't he?"

I didn't answer.

"Of course," she added, "all men do. I wish I could get along without 'em."

I was sitting on a sofa. She came over to sit on the floor near-by, her bleached hair close to my knee. She sighed. "I wish I owned this house."

"Marry the man and own half of it." I put a hand on her

hair and it wasn't nearly as lifeless as I thought it would be. "You could make him happy."

"No," she said. She shook her head and her hair tickled the palm of my hand. "Do you like Al Martino?"

"Not very much. Are you getting ready to tell me what Sylvester wanted from you?"

"I'm thinking about it," she said. "Put your hand in my hair again."

A quickening in me. I rumpled her hair.

From the highway came the sound of a siren, growing, a siren coming our way. It reached a crescendo outside and then grew fainter as it headed north.

"Cops," Mike said.

"Sounded like an ambulance," I said. "Tell me about Sylvester."

She climbed up onto the sofa. "Stop playing detective." She nibbled my ear.

A trap? Pressure in me, in my legs, my loins, my head. Her hair brushed across my face. Her soft hand slid in under my shirt.

A trap? If it was, they had the right bait. She dug her chin into my chest and laughed softly.

"What's funny?" I asked.

"You, probably," she whispered. "I'll bet you're thinking this is going to cost you."

"I'm a poor man," I said, "but attractive. I never pay."

She squirmed higher, her fine breasts flat against my chest. It didn't seem like the right time to ask about Sylvester again. To hell with Sylvester. Her mouth enveloped mine.

Trained? Yes. Would that make it repugnant? Not to me.

She squirmed around again and sat up, her back to me. "This reminds me of high school. Unzip me."

I pulled the tab and the white dress fell away from her smooth shoulders. She stood up and shrugged it off and put it carefully over the arm of a chair.

She reached behind, unhooked her bra, stepped out of her briefs and turned to look at me. "What are you waiting for? This is not a *formal* party, Puma."

I stood up and started to undress. "This sofa's too small," I said.

"The floor is clean," she told me, "and well padded. It's a wonderful floor for frolics."

She was a teaser, giggling, withdrawing, squirming, elusive.

Well, what the hell, it had been her idea; I played it coy, as though none of it really mattered, as though I would just as soon go back to the kitchen for another steak.

She quit playing games then and devoted her skill and imagination to fulfilling her primordial need.

We were still recumbent on the well-padded carpeting when she asked, "Why did you talk about murder before?"

I tried to answer, but didn't quite have the strength.

"What's the matter?" she asked.

I managed to say, "Nothing. I was—thinking. Let me think a moment."

What I wanted was time to regain enough strength to push air through my vocal cords. I took a deep breath and said, "I think your playmates are involved in murder, in the death of Gus Galbini and Marie Veller."

"Galbini?" she asked. "Is that the manager of that fighter, of Terry Lopez?"

"He was."

A few seconds of silence. "I know Terry's wife. I—knew her, I mean—I knew her a little. *About* her, mostly."

"When she got a thousand dollars a night?"

"Poof!" she said scornfully. "Maybe *once*, from some crazy Texan, or something—but nobody gets a thousand regular." A pause. "I've—been on parties with her, back before I met my friend, here, the one who owns this house."

"Don't you go on parties since you met him?"

She frowned. "Well, on dates, like now. But not *parties.*"

I must have looked puzzled, because she explained, "Every girl has dates, like tonight. Even the big movie stars have dates. But *parties*—they're kind of vulgar, my friend told me. I'm too nice a girl for parties, he thinks." She chewed her lip. "That's *love,* isn't it?"

"Hang onto it," I advised her. "He sounds like a prince." I managed to find strength enough to reach the sofa and sit on it.

"Have you got a cigarette on you?" she asked me, and then realized how silly that was. She laughed.

I put on my shorts and went to the kitchen to get my cigarettes. I lighted a pair and came back to hand her one.

"You're nice," she said. "I wish you had a house like my friend. Have you?"

"No, Mike; I'm a poor man."

She sighed. "Most of the nice ones are. It's a silly world, isn't it?"

I nodded.

"That Galbini," she said, "did he marry a chunky girl, a Hunkie?"

"A stocky imitation blonde," I answered. "A Lithuanian. Do you know her, too?"

"I think I've seen her around."

"Is that the girl Sylvester Thornton wanted you to talk about, about Mrs. Galbini?"

A long pause before she shook her head. "Bridget," she said. "Bridget Gallegher. She used to call herself Flame."

"And what did he want you to do about Bridget Gallegher Lopez?"

Silence. A big Diesel went blatting past outside, shaking the house, but silence within.

Finally, she said, "It's not set up, yet. The way it looks, they want to help Terry Lopez get a divorce."

"How?"

"They don't tell me *everything*," she protested. "But the way it looks to me, this Flame has something on her husband and he hasn't got the guts to tell her to go to hell. I guess Terry didn't know about—what his wife used to be. For a chaser, he's sure dumb about his own wife, huh?"

"They often are," I said. "But why should Sylvester want to help Lopez?"

"It's Al who wants to," she said. "I guess Al wants to be Terry's manager, but Terry said no dice until you get rid of Flame. I guess this Terry is real gone on some society dame, or something and he wants a clean divorce, with no beefs from Flame."

"I get it. And what has Bridget Gallegher Flame Lopez got on Terry that Al wants to trade for?"

She shook her head slowly and looked at me candidly. "They didn't say."

Another silence except for the hum of tires from the highway and the faint sound of the surf.

She said quietly, "I'm scared. Do you know who murdered Galbini?"

"Yes," I lied. "When Marie Veller died, I was watching her apartment. I saw her killer leave. It could be and probably is the same person who killed Galbini. But I want to be sure, first."

"You didn't tell the police that," she said. "Why didn't you tell the police? You're not a blackmailer, are you?"

"No. I want to keep it quiet long enough to see if it will lead me to the person who killed Galbini."

"I thought you said it was the same person," she said softly.

"*Probably*," I said. "But I want to be sure."

"Don't tell me the name," she said. "I don't want to know his name. But is it Al Martino?"

"I can't say, Mike. I don't want to get you involved."

"Does Al know you know?" she asked me.

"No, but if he presses you about it, you can tell him I know who the killer of Marie Veller is and I'm not giving it to the police just yet."

She rose. She said, "I'm going to take a shower. I don't want to talk about murder." She picked up her clothes and left the room.

I went into the kitchen and poured myself a cup of coffee and took it back to the living room. If Mike had been sent to trap me, she now had a message to take back to her employers. And even if this adventure had been her idea, they might question her under pressure.

I still hadn't finished my coffee when she came out again, dressed and sweet and clean.

"Watching the lights?" she asked me.

I nodded.

"I like to," she said. "Why is that fun?"

"I don't know, Mike. Ready to go home?"

"I'm not going," she said. "I'm going to stay here. My friend will be back soon. He was due back tonight."

"Ye gods!" I said. "He could have walked in on us and caught us on the floor."

"It wouldn't have mattered," she said. "He's not a gossip."

chapter fourteen

THE OLD TWO-DOOR WENT CHUGGING DOWN THE COAST Highway, as weary as its driver. The intrigues, the hopes, and machinations of all of them went through my fuzzy mind and spelled nothing.

With what I had learned since Mrs. Galbini had come to my office, I should know more than I did. An intelligent operative would have had a case by now, strong enough to take into court. An intelligent operative would have stayed out of the hay and kept his thoughts above the belt. The poor bastard.

They all went around in my mind and made me dizzy, the Lopezes, the Lefkowicses, Delamater, Galbini, Martino, Mueller, Mary, and Doc Golde. And on the periphery, Linda Carrillo and Mike.

I turned off the highway at the ramp north of Wilshire and headed east, toward home. I had screwed my way to nowhere on Mrs. Galbini's time. I had charged her a hundred a day and come up with nothing.

It had been a tiring day, I told myself. My instincts were dulled and my rational mind nonoperative. The threads of the whole cloth were down there in the subconscious, tangled tonight, but tomorrow would be better.

Sleep, Puma, and weave a pattern.

I had half expected to see the Lefkowics limousine waiting in front of my igloo, but the street was bare. I went up and to bed and dreamed of Mike.

I wakened less weary but no less confused. The thought came to me, for some reason, that I didn't *want to know* who killed Gus Galbini. All through breakfast, this unreasonable thought nagged at me.

I was washing an accumulation of two days' dishes when

116

someone pressed the button that activated my melodious two-tone door chime. I went to the door and looked into the unpleasant face of Manny Lefkowics.

"Where's your cousin?" I asked him. "Still fishing?"

"We're not unseparable," he said.

"Its 'in,' not 'un,' Manny. What's on your mind?"

"Mike," he answered. "She here? The boss is worried about her."

I held the door wide. "Come in and look. I slept alone. Why is Al worried?"

He came in, looked around the living room, went to peer into the bathroom and came back to the kitchen, where I now was.

"Al doesn't have to tell you why he's worried, if he is. Where is she, Puma?"

I dried the last dish and closed the cupboard door. I turned to face him. "I don't know. I left her about midnight."

"Where?"

"At the bar in the Shorecrest Hotel."

"What's your interest in her, Puma?"

I shrugged. "I'd say it was about 38-22-37. What's your interest in her, Manny?"

"She didn't come home last night. Did you scare her? Did you tell her to lam?"

"Of course not. You mean she's missing?"

He nodded, studying me.

"Did you notify the police?" I asked him. "This could be serious, Manny."

"Cut out the ham," he said. "You're annoying me again, Puma."

"That's too damned bad," I said. "What am I supposed to do now, tremble?"

Almost imperceptibly, he spread his feet and his broad face was suddenly alert and dangerous. "Last night," he said quietly, "you sounded like you were getting some sense. What's happened since?"

"Last night I was drunk. This morning I'm sober and sour and I hate hoodlums. That's what you are, Manny, a hoodlum. *Beat it.*"

His hand moved quickly and I wasn't armed. His hand moved quickly but not quite as quickly as my foot. To put it as delicately as I can, I kicked out and up, my target the vulnerable area where his legs were joined.

I caught him better than I had any right to hope for. He

shrieked like a woman and doubled in agony and now the
back of his neck was about at a level with my hip.

I chopped down and through and hit the bull's-eye once
more. He crumpled to the linoleum with a thud that rattled
the dishes I had just dried.

I took his gun out of its holster and went to call the police.

Captain Apoyan put his fingers together and looked
thoughtful.

I said, "You look like a merchant about to sell me an
Oriental rug."

He smiled. "Kashan, Bokhara, Ispahan, Sarouk?"

"You're smug," I said. "You won't even rise to an insult.
Why?"

"I'm glad to see you on our side again," he said. "You
wouldn't admit the kidnaping, but now you'll sign an assault
with a weapon complaint. Why?"

"Never mind why, but I've always been on your side. And
you know damned well I have. But when I promise something, the promise is *important,* no matter to whom it's
given. You know, at breakfast I had a feeling I didn't want
to know who killed Galbini. Now I realize why that was."

Captain Apoyan waited patiently, his fingertips still
pressed together.

"I wanted it to be Lefkowics and I knew it wasn't. That's
personal vengeance, isn't it?"

Apoyan nodded slowly and smiled blandly. "And of course
you would never be guilty of *personal* vengeance, would
you?"

I didn't answer.

He said quietly, "Have you considered that this complaint
on Lefkowics is simply your word against his? He claims
you told him to come in and he never took his gun out."

"He has to be punished," I said. "Ask him if he'd rather
I filed a stronger complaint."

Apoyan's eyes narrowed. "Like—kidnaping?"

"I'm not saying. You ask Lefkowics and get his answer.
You tell him it would be best all around if he'd plead guilty
to this morning's charge."

"Now, wait," Apoyan said, quickly. "We're either legal
or—"

"We're just," I finished for him. "You can't prove I'm
doing anything illegal. He's got a lawyer to worry about that.
It's your business to enforce the law, Captain, not interpret
it."

"There are times when I don't like you," he said.

"And other times when you need me," I added. I stood up. "Well, if anyone wants me, I'll be at the office for at least an hour."

"Don't hurry back here," he said. But he winked.

I went out into a real Chamber of Commerce day, clear, clean, and sunny, without a trace of smog, a warm Miami-type day. I wasn't any closer to a solution than I had been last night, but the day made me feel that I was.

At the office, I opened all the windows to let in this wonderful day. Then I sat down to bring my reports up to date. I was steadily typing my way toward my meeting with Mike when the phone rang.

It was Apoyan. "Manny wants to know if you'll settle for assault—*without a weapon.*"

"I don't know. What do you think, Captain?"

"You told me he never got his gun out. You'd have to repeat that in court. You wouldn't lie under oath."

"He'll plead guilty to unarmed assault?"

"Yup."

I accepted that. We take what we can get, on my side of the law. My fingers went back to the machine, building the case up to Mike. When I got to Mike, I would have to improvise; Mrs. Galbini wouldn't be interested in *all* of that interrogation.

I was discreetly through the Mike interrogation and working into this morning's visit from Manny when I heard footsteps in the hall. It could be a patient of Doctor Graves, but I also had the uncomfortable feeling that it could be Manny's belligerent cousin.

I was reaching for my gun when Barney Delamater appeared in my open doorway.

He looked at me blankly. My hand was under my jacket. He said, "You got a gun under there?"

"I was reaching for an eraser," I said lamely. "I can't seem to find it on my desk. Come in."

He came in and sat in my customer's chair. He took out a handkerchief and wiped his bald and perspiring head.

"Nervous, Barney?" I asked him.

"I don't like what's been happening," he admitted. "What's this I hear about Manny Lefkowics?"

"He's pleading guilty to assault. That isn't much."

"And Gus? What have you learned about his death?"

I stared at him, saying nothing.

"Look, Joe," he said pleadingly, "maybe I got on the wrong

side of the fence for a while. But you know I'm no hood-lum."

"You will be, if you keep hanging around with them."

"What can I do, insult 'em? They ask me to a couple poker games, what am I supposed to do?"

"I don't know. I'm not your keeper. What are you here for?"

"I want to know what's going on. First Gus and then Joey Veller's sister— How do we know who's next?"

I smiled at him. "We don't. You thought Martino would take care of me and now you see one of his stooges heading for the clink and you think maybe you joined the wrong side. Right?"

"Nothing like that," he said grimly. "I just wasn't com-fortable with those people."

"All right," I said, "tell me about them, tell me everything you know about them and Galbini and Mueller and Golde and this new organization Martino's trying to set up."

He told me what he knew. None of it was anything I didn't know or hadn't assumed. Lopez would be built up with stumblebums and they were trying to get control of Mueller.

"And Terry's wife?" I asked. "Why the freeze on her? Does she think her husband can make it on his own strength?"

"That's another deal," Barney said. "This Lopez wants a di-vorce, see, but his wife doesn't. That's Martino's job, to get him the divorce."

"I don't follow you."

Barney took a deep breath. "Lopez didn't know about what a—a tramp his wife had been. Now he's in love, I guess." He shrugged. "So Al's getting him grounds."

I kept my gaze on Barney's face and said slowly, "The way I heard it, Bridget Gallegher Lopez has got some kind of bind on Terry. And that's why Al has to scramble."

Barney frowned. "Bind?"

"Something she knows. Something, maybe, she knows that the police would like to know?"

Barney stared at me blankly. "So help me, I never heard that."

I asked, "Who's Terry in love with?"

"I don't know that, either. But I heard it's a big family in this town. You know—society."

"That's what I heard, too," I said. "Barney, you haven't told me anything I don't know."

"I can't help that," he said. "I told you what I know."

We sat there, for a few seconds, in an uncomfortable silence. Half-assed friends, I had called us, and that's the way I felt now; I half trusted him.

He broke the silence, finally. "You don't trust me."

"Not this morning. Maybe later, but not this morning. So long, Barney."

He stood up, stared thoughtfully at me for a couple of seconds, and then went out without saying anything.

I went back to my report—and the phone rang. It was getting to be a busy morning.

The voice of the girl called Mike asked cheerfully, "What are you doing?"

"Sitting here, swamped in nostalgia, reliving the memory of last night."

She chuckled. "Has anyone asked for me?"

"Manny Lefkowics."

A moment's silence, and then, "I'm still at our love nest. My friend went out to get some coffee. He came home right after you left."

A licentious question occurred to me, but I didn't voice it. I asked, "Are you going to stay there for a while?"

"That would be smart, maybe, huh?"

"I think it would. Have you decided not to be an anti-character witness for Flame Lopez?"

A pause. "What have I got against her? She never did me any harm. Right?"

"You're a citizen," I said. "I'm proud to be your friend."

She chuckled again. "I'm going to miss you. I'll have to give you up, Puma; I'm going to marry my friend."

"Wonderful," I complimented her. "He's a lucky man."

"They all were," she said. "Carry on, big boy, and don't lead with your chin." She hung up.

A moment of despondency came to me; the best ones always got married, and not to me. Maybe, if I asked them? No, it would be unfair to the others, so patiently waiting their turn.

I finished the typing and got up to stretch. Everything was there, the dialogues and monologues, the lies and evasions, the truths and half-truths. Everything was there but the answer.

I phoned Captain Apoyan, but he was out to lunch. I got Sergeant Dugan, and asked him: "How about that steak knife? Was it ever identified?"

"Yup. One of a set—owned by the deceased. You figure it."

"Anything else I should know, Marty?"

"Nothing. But maybe you know things we should?"

"I wish I did. I have a feeling something's going to come, though. There's a light about to burst in my brain."

"Okay, swami," he said wearily. "Call us when you light up. We've got a whole damned city to watch."

Every day, they had it, violence and lies, indignant citizens and double-talking politicians and larceny, rape, and child-beating day in, day out. What a life. And we paid them peanuts, screaming about taxes and making the Vegas hoodlums rich.

Citizens: we had no right to the name, a country without shame.

I went out to lunch.

While I ate, I ran them through my mind again, searching for the elusive obvious. The threads began to come unsnarled, ready for the loom. An image began to appear in the pattern, the image of a chaser. Not Puma.

I went back to the office and sat, adding it up. What could I prove? To *know* is one thing; to make it stick in court is far more difficult. Even a confession is meaningless unless a prosecutor can document it. And even documented, how about the jury? They are not always reasonable people, those peers.

I phoned Apoyan to see if he would be in and found out he would be. I went over to the West Side Station and found him in consultation with Dugan.

I spelled it out for them, incomplete as it was, built of hunches and suspicion, reason and lies, a doubtful finger pointing at a doubtful killer.

When I had finished, Apoyan said, "Well, maybe—" Marty Dugan frowned and shrugged. They looked at each other.

Marty said, "I suppose I could run out there and throw my weight around—"

"Let me be the front man," I suggested. "I'll check out what I can the rest of the afternoon and then we'll set it up for tonight, Puma and the Department, working trustingly together."

"You're that sure?" Apoyan asked. "You're going to put that much into a hunch?"

I nodded.

Apoyan looked at Marty again and Marty shrugged again. "What else have we got? It could easily be the way he sees it." His shoulders sagged. "Overtime, it means. All right."

"And don't tell Trask about it," I said. "I want to protect that Carrillo girl as much as possible."

I went out into the bright day and to work.

The neighbors were no help; they weren't nosy neighbors. I finally came face to face with Doc Golde, and he was no help, either. He was going along with the mob until he felt it was safe to pull out. He had not, he told me, ever intended to let Al Martino get any piece of Hans Mueller.

To Marie Veller's neighbors then and no more luck. All these people had been questioned by the police; I had hoped that if they knew something they would be more frank with a private man.

The way it seemed now, the lie I had left with Mike would never leak back to her former playmates. She was entering a new life and she would feel no compulsion to confide in her former friends. So that bit of sneaky Puma deception would probably be wasted. That's what I thought, making my rounds in the sunny afternoon.

At four o'clock I was in Mary Loper's neighborhood, so I stopped in.

"You!" she said. "You were supposed to phone me yesterday afternoon."

"I did, Mary. At three o'clock, just as I promised. And I let the phone ring ten times."

"You couldn't have tried me at three-fifteen, I suppose?"

I didn't answer.

"And last night?" she asked. "At the Western Vista Motel again, no doubt?"

I shook my head.

"You weren't home," she said.

"I was working."

"Huh!"

I sighed.

"To hell with you," she said. "You're *never* around when I need you."

"Simmer down," I said. "We're not married. We're not even engaged. I'm not even leashed. Simmer down."

A silence. The sun flooded the little patio and I closed my eyes against its glare.

"What's the matter?" she asked. "Are you sick?"

"Despondent. I've a job to do tonight that I don't want to do."

"What kind of job?"

I opened my eyes and smiled at her. "A private job. Is there a beer around anywhere?"

"Well!" she said. *"Master* Puma! I'm not a maid."

I continued to smile. "You're not even a maiden. Why do

you have to hate me? Didn't you learn all about me from Mary Pastore? Did you think I was something I'm not?"

She glared at me for seconds and then said wearily, "Get your own damned beer."

I leaned forward on the chaise longue, as though to rise. I groaned and rubbed my back.

"All right, damn it," she said. "Sit there. I'll get it."

In a few minutes she came out from the house again with two cans of beer. We drank in silence.

The beer and the sun soothed her, making her more reasonable. I told her about some of my adventures and Martino's plans.

"And tonight you'll be busy again?" she asked.

"For a while. If I'm through early, should we go and listen to Shearing again?"

"Maybe," she said. "I may be busy. Phone, first."

Dignity, the girl had. And many other charms. I went back to the road, learning nothing, leaving me with my naked hunch, not knowing that Mike had helped in her innocent way.

I ate at Cini's, a 100 per cent Italian dinner. I phoned my answering service from there and learned that Bridget Gallegher (Flame) Lopez had phoned me three times and Mrs. Galbini once.

I phoned the West Side Station and then headed for Westwood.

She opened the door and looked at me doubtfully. "Where's Terry?"

"I don't know, Mrs. Lopez. May I come in?"

"Of course," she said. "I phoned you this afternoon."

"I know." I came into the living room and sat on a love seat. She sat in a near-by chair and stared at me.

I said nothing, waiting for her.

"My husband left about half an hour ago," she said. "To see that girl."

"What girl? The girl you tried to learn about by hiring me?"

She shook her head. "That isn't why I hired you. If it is, why did I fire you? You never found out her name."

"I didn't, did I? Why did you phone me three times this afternoon?"

"I want to know what's going on." She licked her lips. "What am I, an outcast? They're trying to force me out of Terry's life, aren't they, his new *criminal* friends?"

I nodded. "I guess they are. How did you find out?"

"A girl phoned me," she said, "a girl I—used to know. She told me that Thornton wanted her to tell Terry some—nasty things about me, but she wasn't going to do it."

I said, "Terry's kind of innocent, isn't he? And still, he's not exactly a Boy Scout."

She said nothing, staring at me as though trying to read my mind.

I said, "What else did Mike tell you?"

She didn't answer.

I leaned back in the love seat. "I should have realized, when you were so quick to be Terry's alibi, that an alibi works two ways. If he was with you, then you were with him, each covering the other."

She said nothing.

"I should have realized," I went on, "that when Terry suffered the worst humiliation of his career—*and didn't come home to you*, you'd realize this new girl was not just a passing fancy."

"What's her name?" she asked.

"It doesn't matter. If anyone would know her name, though, it would be Gus Galbini, wouldn't it? Though you probably went to Galbini's love nest expecting to find Terry and the girl. Instead, you found Gus. You tried to force him to tell you where Terry was. He probably told you that if you didn't leave Terry alone, he'd tell Terry about your background. It might even be grounds for divorce, your not telling Terry about your background."

Her bosom rose and fell. She stared at me as though in shock.

"Where did you get the gun?" I asked her.

She ignored the question. She said, "You weren't watching Marie Veller's place. That was a trap, telling Mike that, wasn't it?"

I shook my head.

"If you *knew*," she said, "you'd have told the police. You always work with the police."

"Always," I agreed. "Right up to the second it starts to cost me money."

"Blackmail," she said hoarsely.

I said nothing.

"What's the girl's name?" she asked. "It's a big name, isn't it? It's probably a name somebody would pay to keep clean, keep out of the papers."

"Possibly," I agreed. "Was it an accident, your killing Gus? Did you take the gun along, hoping to use it on Terry's girl and then use it to threaten Gus, to get her name from Gus?"

A pause, and then, "I don't have any money. But there's money to be made here, somewhere in this mess. You'd know how to milk it, wouldn't you?"

"Was it an accident?" I asked again. "Where's the gun?"

"They're trying to get rid of me," she said softly, "and you want to help them. You! I thought you hated hoodlums. You're working for them, right now, aren't you?"

I shook my head. "How much money did Marie Veller want?"

She stared at the floor.

"Miss Veller," I went on, "knew what you were. So she was armed when you came over, armed with a knife. But she was no match for you, was she?"

She looked up, her chin high. "If you saw me there, you'd know where I parked the car. Where was that?"

I paused, and played a hunch. "I didn't see your car. I didn't see any car. I saw you, though. And I have a fat hunch that Marie Veller told Mrs. Galbini a few things, though I can't prove it, yet."

"Why didn't you see my car, if I was there?" She paused. "Didn't you follow me?"

"Why? I was watching the apartment from a distance, watching *everybody* who came and went. How was I to know you had killed her?"

"I didn't," she said. "I never killed anybody, never."

I shrugged, and stood up. "So, okay. I've nothing to sell, then, and I'd better take what little I have down to the West Side Station."

Fear in her eyes. She started to say something, and stopped.

"And maybe you'd better come along," I added, "just so you won't have a chance to get rid of the gun, in case you haven't already. Come on; we'll go in my car."

"You're not a policeman," she said.

I took out my gun and held it on her. I went over to pick up the phone.

"Wait," she said quickly. "That won't help *anybody*. Please sit down, Mr. Puma."

I stood where I was. "An accident? I can't cover for a cold-blooded killer, not at any price. But an accident—"

She stared at the floor again. A long pause, and then, "He tried to take the gun away from me. It was an accident. And so was—"

But I said quickly, "Quiet! I think I heard somebody out in front. It might be Martino. Don't move now; I'll go." I went to the door, my gun still in my hand.

I opened the door and said to Marty Dugan, "Okay. Take

her. I don't want to face her, right now. I'll see you at the station."

Apoyan looked at the clock over my head and said, "I've still got time to get home for the Paar show. They found the gun. In a flower pot, yet, under a rubber plant. Amateurs—"
I said nothing.
"Why so gloomy?" he asked quietly.
"I helped 'em. Those stinking, lousy hoodlums—I did 'em a favor."
"And us," he added. "We're not hoodlums. You can't make it personal, Joe. You do your job and hope for the best."
"She hasn't any money," I said, "and damned few friends. What kind of lawyer can she get?"
Apoyan sighed. "The best, unfortunately. Miss Carrillo is paying for the lawyer. *Anonymously.* Now, what kind of deal is that? Can you understand women, Joe? If anybody should, you should."
"I can't," I said, "and I don't want to. It would spoil their charm." I stood up. "Well, I've got a date to hear Shearing. I'll see you in the morning, Captain."
"Right. Sleep soundly, now, Joe."
"Sure," I said. "Hell, yes."
But I knew I wouldn't.

Printed in the United States
By Bookmasters